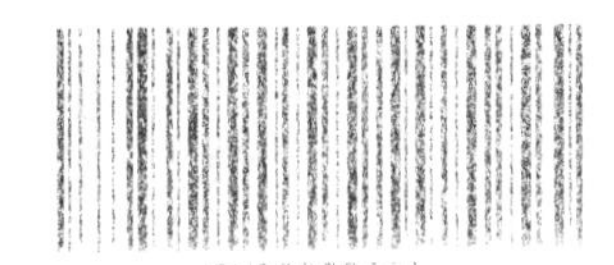

NO SURRENDER

NO SURRENDER

A Story of Angola

James Watson

LONDON
VICTOR GOLLANCZ LTD
1991

Acknowledgement

For their generous help in sharing with me their knowledge of Angola, I wish to thank Jane Bergerol, Marga and Tana Holness and Jane Morgan.

JW

First published in Great Britain 1991
by Victor Gollancz Ltd
14 Henrietta Street, London WC2E 8QJ

British Library Cataloguing in Publication Data
Watson, James *1936–*
No surrender.
I. Title
823.914 [F]

ISBN 0-575-04893-X

Photoset in Great Britain by
Rowland Phototypesetting Ltd, Bury St Edmunds, Suffolk
and printed by St Edmundsbury Press Ltd,
Bury St Edmunds, Suffolk

Author's Note

The action of this story takes place immediately prior to two momentous events in Southern Africa, in November 1989 and February 1990—free elections in Namibia, making independence from South African dominance possible for the Namibian people; and the release from 27 years' imprisonment in South Africa of Nelson Mandela, leader of the African National Congress.

The focusing of world attention on such developments might easily obscure the dark history leading up to these events, not only in Namibia and South Africa but in the so-called Front Line states, in particular Mozambique and Angola.

The apartheid republic of South Africa has repressed its own Black people. Less well known are its attempts to destabilise the nations on its borders. For over a quarter of a century the people of Angola suffered invasions by the armies of South Africa, but in the West very little of this 'hidden war' was reported.

The People's Republic of Angola has long posed a threat to South Africa: first, it is a socialist country; second, it is a multi-racial society. Devastated by war and economic difficulties, Angola is nevertheless rich in natural resources. It is an example of what the nation states of Africa *might* become—prosperous, free from exploitation, creating present and future in a spirit of sharing, justice and racial harmony.

Officially South African invasions of Angola have been denied. Air attacks and border incursions have been explained away as 'defensive measures'. Meanwhile, UNITA guerrillas armed and financed by South Africa and the United States of America have terrorised the population —by kidnapping, destroying crops, killing cattle, looting, raping, beating, mutilating; laying mines along roads and in fields; burning villages to ash.

Wherever possible UNITA forces have avoided FAPLA, the army of Angola, preferring to massacre unarmed villagers and then vanish into the bush with hostages whom they have forced to fight against their own people.

Despite the terror; despite the lack of food, widespread damage to transport, industry and power supplies, the Angolan people have shown amazing resilience. They not only continue the struggle of life, they laugh at their suffering. They possess next to nothing, but what they possess, they share. Not the least of their gifts is an extraordinary capacity to joke at their predicament.

This courage united with optimism has enabled the people of Angola to resist the forces arraigned against them. It promises to carry them through whatever grim days continue to lie in wait for them.

It is to the people of Angola that this book is dedicated.

Homage to Angola

Bear witness to these,
The casualties of hope.
These queues of the limbless,
The orphans, the starving.

Their resistance has seen off
The usurper; defied the hot steel
Of the invader.

Their faith trounces sorrow.
They say, 'We have nothing
But our teeth', yet their smile
Lights the valley of shadows.

From sufferings shared
Love takes root; and hope
Returns as the forest wind.

MALENGA NAKALE

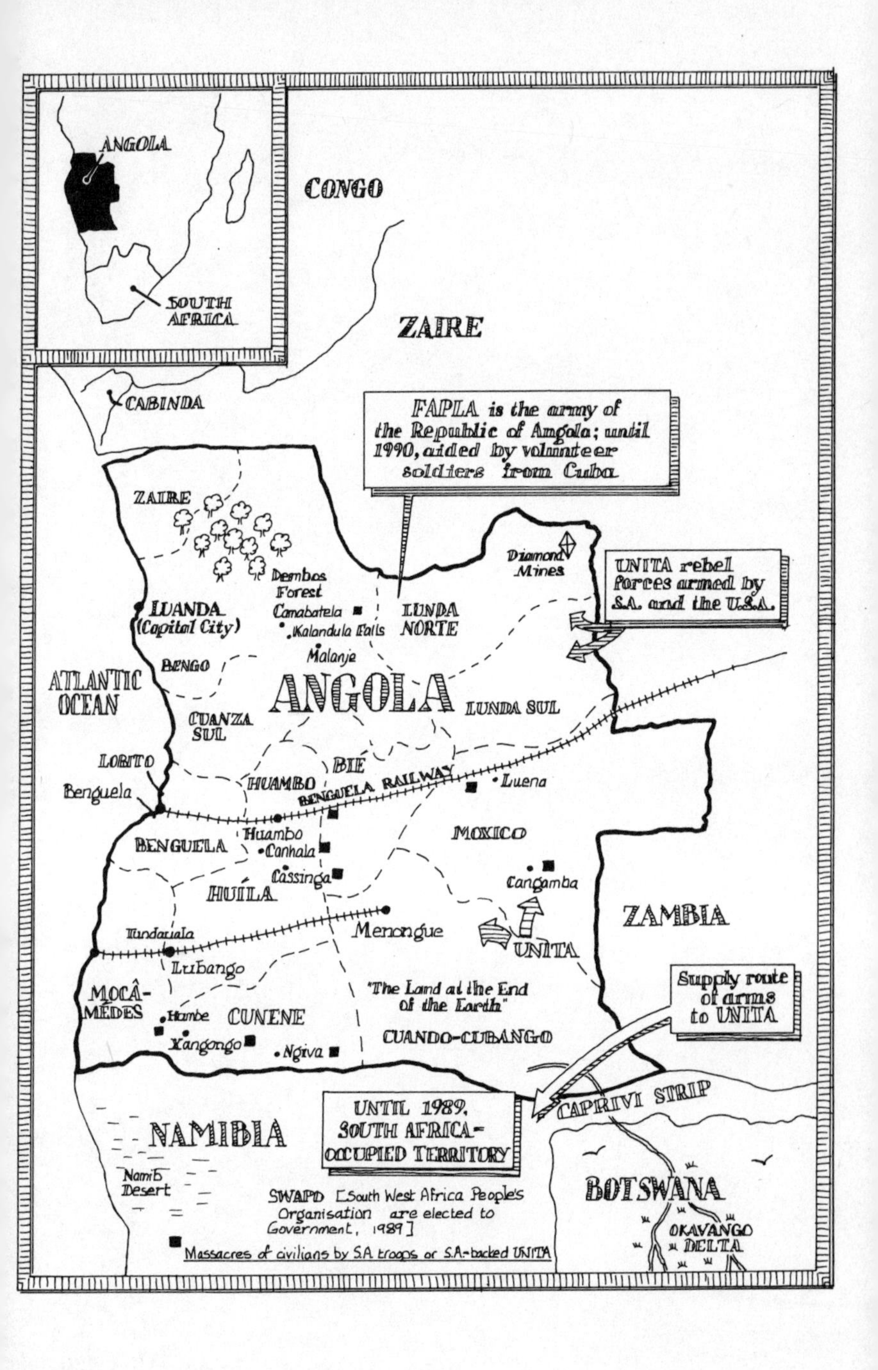
ANGOLA
SOUTH AFRICA
CONGO
ZAIRE
CABINDA
FAPLA is the army of the Republic of Angola; until 1990, aided by volunteer soldiers from Cuba
ZAIRE
Dembos Forest
Diamond Mines
UNITA rebel forces armed by S.A. and the U.S.A.
LUANDA (Capital City)
Camabatela
Kalandula Falls
LUNDA NORTE
Malanje
BENGO
ATLANTIC OCEAN
ANGOLA
LUNDA SUL
CUANZA SUL
LOBITO
BIE
HUAMBO
BENGUELA RAILWAY
Luena
Benguela
BENGUELA
Huambo
Canhala
MOXICO
Cassinga
Cangamba
HUILA
ZAMBIA
Tundavala
Menongue
UNITA
Lubango
Supply route of arms to UNITA
"The Land at the End of the Earth"
MOÇÂ-MEDES
Hambe
CUNENE
Xangongo
Ngiva
CUANDO-CUBANGO
CAPRIVI STRIP
UNTIL 1989, SOUTH AFRICA-OCCUPIED TERRITORY
NAMIBIA
Namib Desert
BOTSWANA
SWAPO [South West Africa People's Organisation are elected to Government, 1989]
OKAVANGO DELTA
Massacres of civilians by S.A troops or S.A-backed UNITA

Prologue

LONDON, 2.30 p.m.

"Angola?—impossible. We do not send youth volunteers to that country. Most of Africa, but not there, I'm afraid."

"Why not?"

"Because it is a country at war. The UNITA rebels have killed thousands of civilians. And the country is overrun with murder squads. We could not permit you to take the risk."

"That is where I want to serve."

"Merely because you were born there?"

"No."

"Then why?—heavens, young lady, Angola's the forgotten nation."

"It is a wonderful country."

"Wonderful it may be—the Tundavala Falls—beautiful! But its people are starving. Don't tell me you think you can rescue them from their fate single-handed?"

"Of course not."

"Even great nations can do nothing to save her."

"I don't think great nations are trying to."

"That's our final decision."

"If you don't send me to Angola I shall make my own way there somehow."

"We've placements in Ghana, Nigeria, Malawi . . ."

"Angola or nothing!"

"Know the name, soldier, for those who try to duck their duties to the nation?"

"I am not a traitor, Sir. But I am against war and fighting."

"You've a yellow streak down your back longer than a crocodile's tail; a disgrace to your Scottish ancestry. Get this clear, every true-born South African male has a duty to protect his homeland."

"Yes."

"You agree with me, then?"

"But South Africans shouldn't invade other people's homelands."

"I don't know what you mean, soldier."

"Or shoot their people in cold blood."

"No national servicemen are given such orders."

"I was forced to bury the dead."

"That is not official information . . . Listen, we are not without understanding. We do not wish to penalise our own kind, not unless we have to. You give me your word that you won't attempt another bunk and . . ."

"Send me to stand guard somewhere in the great Okavango Delta, Sir, where there are only birds and fish—and I'll give you my word."

"Ten days extra duties . . . Now get out of my sight!"

Chapter One

Tomas possesses all the skills—trapping, dribbling, passing; and he can shoot with either foot. That is why Malenga has two extra players on her side.

She calls, "Pass it, Salu!" Her six-year-old centre-back attempts to speed the ball on its way by using both feet at once. Ball and player crash into the sand at the halfway line—between a string of washing, sun-scrubbed and dazzling, and the new Medical Centre.

"OK—mine!" The ball is with Malenga. She takes to the wing, overkicking a forward pass which threatens to run into the bush. The shadows are emerald dark here, and the sand green with oncoming dusk.

Tomas hurls out of his goal towards her. "Watch out for Maradona!" He collides with her outstretched palm. "Foul—free kick."

"For me, you mean?"

"No, you fouled me, Sis."

"Tell that to the referee."

"We don't have a referee."

"Well, then . . ." They stand six paces apart, she tall, wide-shouldered, long-armed, in jeans cut to knee length, wearing a loose shirt of scarlet; he in khaki trousers too big for him, taken from a dead bandit by the river: Tomas of the Nine Lives.

"Try saving a penalty instead."

Tomas has no time for rules. He enjoys penalties. He takes up a crouching position between goalposts which also don't conform to the rules—one is his back-pack (which contains everything he owns), the other is his hunting gun.

As Malenga wonders whether to slice her shot with the outstep or curl it across goal with her instep, she is suddenly called for.

From the fields beyond the village, beyond the schoolhouse at the village edge—an explosion. The ground quivers. One blast, everybody running.

"Bandits!"

Malenga runs, then halts, uncertain. "Doctor Garcia—we must fetch him." Brain and feet equally slow; stupid. It's shock.

Tomas has retrieved his gun and back-pack. He comes towards Malenga Nakale, trainee medic and schoolmarm. In English now, "We not dilly dally, Sis."

Her doubts she carries with her, expunging them in speed: two human arrows towards the smoke over the bushes, to the corner made by the giant baobab tree.

In the fields the women have been working the last hour of daylight. Now they converge upon a screaming.

Until now there's been singing, and the women's voices have been answered by the tune of the cicadas and answered again deep in the bush by the frog battalions along the river banks.

"Ma-lenga! Ma-lenga!" The crowd of women opens for her. Tomas checks her progress for an instant. His face is screwed up, one hand half-covering his eyes.

"It's Dédo!"

Stood on a mine.

Salu's sister; bright star of Malenga's class.

Beside a cluster of cedars, in their lengthening shadow, Déodora had been hoeing rich, red earth. Everyone knows —mines are to be expected: the last of the war.

"Tomas—go get the Doctor. Salu—black bag please, from the Centre—hurry!" Malenga kneels in hot soil; red soil soaked with red. "Don't let her look. Hold her head, and her hands. Good. Soothe her. Cool her." The women obey, all eyes on Dédo's face, averted from her terrible injury.

The girl's left foot is a bloody pulp. "You stop bleeding, Sis," instructs Tomas.

"I thought I told you . . ."

"I fetch Garcia. Fast." She wishes she could do the racing away, the plunging into the bush. She looks down at the leg, writhing.

The foot's severed. Stop the bleeding.

Malenga pictures Tomas go, sprinting down the slope from the village, down the burning yellow track which leads to the river, where Doctor Leon Garcia has gone—today of all days—to treat a sick worker on the bridge project.

She's tugged off her shirt: red to red; places it over the leg, the stump. "Stretcher—we must get her to the Centre. Dédo, listen. I'm doing what I can. You'll be fine."

Salu brings the medical case Garcia has been putting together for Malenga, of worn black leather, wide-based, with a tough steel clasp.

Under the leg, fragments of mine. She scrapes them away. Treat for shock. In the past few weeks she's watched over Garcia's shoulder. "Your turn will come, Malenga."

"I'm not ready."

"You've the gift."

But do I have the nerve? Dédo fights to sit up. Her face

is stretched, swollen. Her scream is aimed at Malenga's heart.

"Keep her flat."

From the medical case she takes a roll of cloth, stronger than a bandage. Old Maria has hobbled up from the village. The very breath of her is a comfort. "See, Maria's arrived. That's good news."

The old woman presses her way between weepers. Nothing new in the world for her, a veteran of all the wars in this ravaged land. She places a soft thatch of fingers over the screaming mouth. Maria of the Old Magic, and it works. "There, there, child. Choko the Wise One will bring you sleep."

The morphine stays momentarily in Malenga's hand. Morphine, the killer of pain. Tempted. She rejects it: not for children. She chooses to work the bandage three times around the limb below the knee.

"Stick, Salu, yes—something straight and strong." Salu hunts. It is his beautiful sister who lies screaming. He finds. Malenga thanks him in Tuga—Portuguese. She calls him Little Brave One. He shuts off his tears.

Things are beginning to work: fingers, eyes; lazy brain is in gear. "Hold her other leg, Salu."

"Prepare," Garcia always says. "Rehearse your actions in your head."

Thanks, Doctor, and where are you?

Malenga thrusts the stick into the tourniquet of cloth and slowly, slowly twists it, tightens it. Sweat drips from the end of her nose, drips from her arms, seeps through fingers. Must clamp off. Someone is drying her. She nods.

The interior of the medical case delivers up one haemostat, a pair of locking tongues, scissors-like, gleaming.

No alternative—the foot's gone.

Hospital?—three hundred kilometres away; transport?—nil; communications?—there'll be a telephone next year, terrorists permitting.

Garcia: "The mines aren't intended to kill, but to maim, to take out the workers: no work, no wealth!"

Arteries first; powerful spurts, timed with the pulse. Tomas, what's keeping you?

Water has been brought. It is offered to Dédo, calm now, fading. "No drink. Doctor's orders." Malenga works at the exploded leg, at the arteries. No to drink, no to antiseptic too. Not in a deep wound.

Rehearse, yes. The tourniquet will have to be removed shortly. She is tying off. The stretcher has arrived. In the corner of her eye, a metallic glint. Salu is holding the leftovers of the mine.

She is up, stiff, swaying, steadied by Old Maria. For a moment in the turn of the light, the rectangle of steel held by Salu resembles one of those old catechisms hand-stitched and placed in a frame above the bed. Salu traces the lettering with his fingers. He has just begun to read. His catechism for the day shines clear and bronze in the falling sun. In English, it says—FRONT TOWARD THE ENEMY.

Doctor Garcia had taken the one bicycle belonging to the Medical Centre, so Tomas runs. First scrub, then bush, then trees obliterating the sky. One of the engineers had stepped on a snake. "Bad medicine!" laughed Garcia before rushing off.

No sounds come from the bridge works, no hammering, no singing. Tomas stops. Too hot for mist this early: could it be smoke ahead?

Something wrong.

Walking now, breathless but not with running; with fear as the path narrows, the ground drops. The air smells of river.

His short cut will soon hit the newly surfaced dirt-track through the clearing to the bridgehead. After the bridge, the road is even better. One day there will be tarmac and the kimbo—the refugee village—will have its very own name.

At this point the river banks are reached unexpectedly. The trees halt. A few paces farther on the ground forms craters several metres across—shell holes recalling the last invasion by the Boers.

The village kids swim in the largest of the craters, for it is safer than the river. "We must count our blessings," Garcia had said. "The South Africans dug us our swimming pool!"

After the craters, the shore flattens into reed banks. Where the ground is firmest stands the steel-box bridge.

Silent and empty.

Tomas feels his sweat dry cold. He clutches his hunting gun. He is the village hunter. Official. He brings down antelope: he ought not to be afraid. Across the bridge is the doctor's bike, neatly propped against a girder.

The spirits have deserted this place. Choko the Wise One has flown to his favourite motsaudi tree somewhere between earth and heaven; his snoozing hour.

Could the bite of a snake make everyone vanish?

Tomas decides he will have to cross. That way he will get a fuller view of the river, its widening, its bending. There is more light in the centre though the sun has long since slithered between the branches of the trees.

More light, yes, criss-crossed by the spars of the bridge. Tomas notices the old bullet marks. Over seventy died here.

Later, FAPLA—the People's Army—made things safe. And the treaty of peace should have ended all that.

He gazes up river and down, then at both banks. He watches the slow shift of brown water. His attention reverts to the far bank, checking it section by section.

Tomas sees bodies among the reeds.

"Drop the gun, kid—and don't move!" He is addressed not in his own language, Tuga, but in English. Thanks to his adoptive sister's careful instruction, Tomas understands every word.

He obeys. He half turns, raises his hands. Four AK-47s—Kalashnikovs—are directed at his head. The soldiers are in the uniforms of the UNITA bandits, yet three of the four are white.

Tomas, you are a dead man.

"You speakee English, boy?"

He is caged, his back-pack snatched from his shoulder. The tallest soldier, the Black in the party, is not that much older than Tomas—nineteen at most. He picks up Tomas's gun by the barrel.

"Real pop-gun, Boss!" He swings it round his head and releases it in the direction of the reeds; of the bodies.

"Damn it, Sparkler, they pay good money for antiques like that back in Durban."

"Sorry, Boss. You want me fetch?"

"Forget it." Boss is short, neck and sideburns close-shaven. In his forage cap he wears an exotic feather, black tinged with scarlet. Around the band are pinned badges of film stars. What catches Tomas's attention most are ammunition belts strung crosswise over his shoulders, one containing bullets, the other stuffed with cassettes for the Sony Walkman clipped to his middle.

The eyes of Boss have the look of fever in them, and the black mud pressed around them accentuates their brilliant and piercing blueness.

"English I much good."

"Say 'Sir', shrimp-ass."

"Sir."

Tomas's back-pack has been emptied with a shake.

"Any blue movies, Cardinal?"

The oldest of the soldiers, wearing sergeant's stripes, is grey, stone-faced. He picks up the English-Portuguese dictionary given to Tomas by Malenga. Papers slip from the pages.

Malenga's poems.

Tomas forgets he is supposed to have his hands in the air. He gathers the sheets before they can be wafted into the river by the careless breath of evening.

"Give!" Boss holds the rank of captain. He examines the papers. "Bloody poetry, comrades . . . And in English. Did you write this crap, boy?"

Tomas nods. "Just me only."

"Just you only. Not nobody else?"

"No, not nobody."

"Very curious, because this stuff's actually grammatical." He sings out the lines:

I stand back from the river of blood
And discover sweet words.
They restore me like a fountain
Sprung from the desert.

"Mussolini?" The third of the white soldiers comes from behind Tomas, salutes Boss. Once powerfully-built, he has fattened with age. He is double-chinned, his arms bulge from his combat jacket, his stomach spills from baggy khaki trousers; patched, muddied.

"Boss?"

"Show this kid what the White Wolves do to liars."

Tomas is yanked high in the air, jammed against the spars of the bridge. One bang shunts out his breath, another will shatter his bones.

Boss, the captain, signals an end to Tomas's correction. "Let that be a lesson to you, Not Nobody. Lie to us, to Crowbar*, and Crowbar smash tiny skull—savvy?"

Cardinal: "It's getting dark, Boss. We have orders."

As if to remind Cardinal that he is a subordinate, Boss takes his time, chooses to scour the rest of the poem. He grunts with disapproval. "This stuff's heresy . . . it doesn't even bloody rhyme . . . What's your opinion, Fat Man?"

Sweltering, disgruntled, exhausted, suffering from a septic leg, Musso very nearly groans aloud with frustration. He wants to say, Get on with it, Boss—kill the kid. He summons a gob of phlegm. He spits. "Bloody pacifism, Boss."

"But very female, wouldn't you say?" Boss is smiling. "We're home and dry, I think, comrades."

He screws up the sheaf of poems, tosses it into the river. Tomas watches the current take them away. On the surface of the water, the poems unfold like lilies.

Boss's mind has switched back to duty. He snatches Tomas by the hair, spins him in the direction of the village. "Now lead us to your poet, Not Nobody."

* Crowbar: nickname of a notoriously brutal unit of the South African military, the Koevoet (pronounced Koofort).

Chapter Two

"What can have happened to them, Maria?"

From here, at the edge of the village, where the new Medical Centre has been erected, the silence is gently shaken by the call of owls; that and the troubled breathing of Dédo.

Another of the mutilated. Malenga had witnessed hundreds of them at the airport on her arrival, in the streets of Luanda, the capital, and later in Benguela; queuing down the corridors of bomb-damaged hospitals.

"You ought to rest, my child," advises Maria. "I'll watch her."

Child. Can't remember when I was last called a child. It's comforting but I must not be a child.

Malenga has done all she can. The bleeding has been staunched. She has cleaned the wound, bandaged it. Dédo yesterday won the long jump in the kimbo Olympics. Last week she won the reading prize and shared the prize for sums with Tomas.

Now she is dying.

"The pain, Malenga."

"It will go away, Dédo." Hand clutched, Dedo's nails biting into her palm.

"The doctor?"

"*Em breve*—soon." She's shivering, sliding away from us. Malenga gets up. "Another blanket." She takes one of two oil lamps, crosses the dispensary, pauses at the window. "We shall have visitors."

Maria spreads the extra blanket over Dédo. "There—Choko says sleep."

"If she can just last the night."

Maria leans into the lamplight, shakes her head. A year ago her husband was taken into the forest by UNITA bandits. His body was never found. Her two sons had joined the government army. The elder had been killed in Lunda Norte during FAPLA's campaign to release villagers from the terror of UNITA attacks. The younger son had died at the battle of Cuito Kuanavale, where the tide of the South African invasions had been finally turned.

The smell of newly-sawn wood mingles with the odour of disinfectant and cold scents from the forest. Sleep heals, Malenga's mother Fransina used to say.

"Things not going as you'd hoped, Child?" Ah yes, Fransina used the word; not often—too busy.

"At least I'm doing what you'd approve of . . . at last."

"You're a Nakale. It was inevitable."

Nakale: a name to be conjured with—something Malenga's least-favourite teacher, Mrs Trench, had pointed out. Yes, Mrs Trench, but not one I really want to live with. Dozing, head on hands, cold.

I suddenly shiver
At memories of unwelcome
In a cold, harsh past.

How strange all those London names sound now—Bethnal Green, Camden Town, Pimlico; and later, where England and Wales meet, snow halfway up the school gates, shin-deep across the playing fields.

Here are warm words, warm names, and more beautiful —Huambo, Moxico, Huila. Peaceful names. Riddled with shells, spattered with bullets in the war without ending.

If only people could see the Great Plateau at dawn.

The day's second explosion, mightier though muffled by forest, announces the death of the box-girder bridge. No trade will pass this way, no progress, till the beleaguered government finds the funds, till there are engineers to replace those who lie with their throats cut at the river's edge.

It is called: destabilisation.

Already the villagers are abandoning their homes, fading on silent footsteps along well rehearsed routes to concealment; swiftly, automatically—naturally.

"You too, Child." Malenga does not need to be told the reputation of UNITA. "I'll stay—they'll want none of the old and dying."

Would like to. Good sense says, live to fight another day. Then why am I shaking my head? "She's my patient, Maria. I'm being paid, too." She lowers her cheek on to Dédo's forehead. "And she's my friend."

Maria does not argue, but she is not impressed. "And you already gave up such a good life, Child."

"It was no life, Maria."

"And this?"

On the night flight to Luanda, the stewardess had asked, "Holiday?"

Oh no. "I've left England for good." Last images still resting on the inner eye: the quilted fields of Sussex and Kent, the white cliffs, Sealink ploughing the waves. "It's no place any longer—not for the young." Then the burnished domes of Sophia; and Lagos, the first great terminal of Africa.

"I see."

Malenga doubted it, for she understood so little herself. Later she wrote a poem in the airport lounge, about the bitterness she had felt that grey English winter, and the decision she had made against all advice, to do Voluntary Service in the land of her birth; a land which was a total stranger to her.

From the plush comfort
Of the Protocol lounge
My first vision of home:
Queues of the limbless
Snaking into the dark.

Somebody is out there. "Our guests have arrived, Maria." She feels their presence as the UNITA bandits approach the steps of the Medical Centre.

This semblance of calm is almost convincing—but the semblance is broken open by a voice calling her name:

"Malenga Nakale?—Nakale!"

Her first thought: they've got Tomas—but would he tell them her name? Never.

The entrance door is kicked open. Malenga has reached for an oil lamp, raised it. Hands in the air, Tomas has been prodded up three of the four Medical Centre steps, a shield in the event of a gunshot from the interior of the Centre.

"Step out!" Boss thrusts Tomas aside, still holding him by the crop of his neck.

Stunned, Malenga hears herself playing for time. "The doctor is not here."

"Malenga Nakale?"

She remembers her training in Benguela, from Nose the kindly giant. "No . . . not my name."

"Tell that to the cuckoos." Boss pins her against the doorpost. "More liars, Musso."

"Enkale is my name!"

Musso locks himself round her. The captain enters, crosses the room towards Dédo. Ignoring Maria, he uses the lamp to give himself a glimpse of the wounded girl. His words are for Malenga. "Get packed, Doll. Toothbrush, sanitary towels . . . But no bloody poetry!"

"Who are you?"

"They call me Zorro. It's all you need to know." He is through into the room where records are kept. This time Nose would not be proud of her: you should have destroyed everything.

Zorro re-emerges with a buff envelope. "Your Cuboid doctor thinks a lot of you, Nakale."

She stands her ground, yet feels the hopelessness of her position. "The doctor went to the river, he—"

"The doctor's gone to hell, lady. With some others of his persuasion." He almost pushes the lamp into her face. "What shall we call her, Fat Man?"

"He's choking me."

"Educated at a private school in little ole England—ha! Got GCSEs, have you?" Zorro looks her over: handsome, proud. "So you think you're the Queen of Sheba, right?"

"Sheba, Boss—that's a good name."

Taking Old Maria's advice, Malenga had changed out of short-cut jeans into cotton trousers. She wears a thin wool highneck sweater and sleeves reaching to her wrists.

She has not been able to disguise her handsomeness.

"I don't want anybody tampering with this dame, understand, Fat Man?"

Musso is more interested in the discomfort of his septic leg. "If she's a nurse, Boss . . ."

Malenga notices the tee-shirt Zorro wears beneath his

open combat jacket. It says in brash letters, KILLING IS OUR BUSINESS—AND BUSINESS IS GOOD. "Treat him, Nakale. And Sparkler out there. He's got the shits . . . Fifteen minutes, then we march!"

I'm bandaging one of your killers, Doctor. Because you would do the same. This Zorro has found the photo of your family. Thrown it in the bin. No comment. I would like to kill him. He has condemned everything here. Nothing will survive.

They've beaten Tomas but I'm not allowed to treat him till I've finished the others. Sparkler is about my age. All he can wait for is setting the kimbo alight.

"Right, Grandma," Zorro says to Maria. "Help nursey get this kid out of here."

Malenga: "She mustn't be moved."

"She'll not last till morning . . . Shift her, Grannie."

Cardinal helps. The bed tilts over the Centre steps. Dédo awakes. "Malenga!"

"Out!"

Musso laughs as Malenga struggles. "Wildcat, Boss!" His strength is twice hers.

"You Zulus never learn, do you?" Zorro has picked up Tomas, carts him out, pitches him down the steps. To act is to destroy.

Malenga takes her chance. In Tuga, "Tomas, when I shout FAPLA—you run!"

He knows. He is a witness. He will die.

Sparkler lives up to his name: a detonation and the new Medical Centre also dies. The roof falls in upon flames, the walls burst outwards. The sturdy poles supporting the verandah are blown sideways.

Taking their cue from the Mighty Zorro, the White Wolves applaud as fire feeds fire, as the dispensary becomes a firework display of precious medicines. The flames soar above the roof of the forest.

"Dédo?" Malenga leans over Déodora, shielding her from the intensity of the heat. "These men are going to take me. I promise, I'll be back. Maria will nurse you better."

She almost misses the whispered reply, "I love you," yet catches the child's hand. "That goes for me too." She squeezes the hand. And there's Tomas she loves. He is a silhouette against the fire, watching.

Now! She turns. At the top of her voice, she shouts:

"FAPLA!"

Even through the stereo earphones he has donned, to accompany the sweet sight of destruction, Zorro registers the one word which sends guerrillas and infiltrators, mercenaries or secret killer squads, diving for cover.

FAPLA, the People's Army, has turned back the most powerful invasions in the history of Africa, driven the Boer regiments off Angolan soil. Now their task is to mop up the bandits—bandits like these—who terrorise the remoter parts of this vast country.

"FAPLA!" And pointing away past the football pitch to the end house of the village. At the same time—thanks for the tip, Nose—Malenga drops on to her knees as if expecting a burst of gunfire.

Tomas runs.

"Boa sorte!" Good luck, little brother.

Watch out for Maradona.

Musso and Sparkler try to shoot the soccer star as he darts for goal, switching course, dodging invisible defenders.

"I think I plugged him, Boss," claims Musso.

Not Maradona.

She waits for Zorro. She is shaking. His fury is cold, expressionless. He has been made to take cover, fooled. Worse, he has been obliged publicly to show his respect for the People's Army.

"You disturbed my music, Sheba." The White Wolves make space. He may shoot her, or merely slash her face.

Cardinal, risking his own skin, speaks. "Remember our mission, Boss."

"Sparkler?"

"Boss?"

A gesture is enough: the kimbo must die.

"Miss Nakale, you and I are not going to get on."

The village is aflame.

Despite the two hours' marching through the bush, Malenga is ice. No, not ice—wood. Numb as wood. And I am snapping like wood. She had asked, "Where are you taking me?"

Silence.

Wood, yes—but iced wood, and the ice is seeping through my veins. There is a four-letter word for it—fear. Now I know what writers mean when they talk about nerves 'jangling'.

To be kidnapped, and alone among wolves.

Any advice, Nose?

You're on your own now.

I thought you'd say that. My father Julius would: a test of character, eh, Dad?

Hold on to things—faces: Tomas, Salu, Eli, orphans all; in Benguela, Nose, laugh like a waterfall; in Luanda, Eve of the Women's Organisation ('The next war, comrades, is against our menfolk, to grant us equality in everything!'); or the singer, Carlos, praising Malenga's poetry ('But it is too sad—there's so little joy in it . . .').

True. That's because there's been so little joy in me.

Give me time. It was happening here. Something warm and wonderful. Now this. Goodbye Dédo, farewell Garcia.

Once more, I am alone.

Como vai isso? How's life with you? Don't ask, I walk the precipice with no moon to guide me; and I can only guess it's because of you, my famous father.

"Malenga Nakale?"

They knew me. This has been no accident. I am what Cardinal called their mission.

Sunrise, heatrise. Zorro announces, "We kip at noon." One mouthful of water spared for the prisoner. Nothing to eat.

Eventually Sparkler appeals for mercy. "Boss—I gotta shit."

"OK, take twenty. Sheba, give him some more of that crap-stopper." She has been permitted to bring the medical case. "And check Musso's bandage."

Zorro's route has led along high ground, following the course of the river. All week Malenga has been teaching her class geography. They prefer stories, but she persisted: "You've got to know about your own country."

"Why, Miss?"

"Because it's full of such gorgeous names."

Everything you think and say marks you as the outsider.

After the forest, there will be scrubland, the landscape swelling up through the trees, opening out to the sun. The dry ground will be populated with deep-rooted acacia and shepherd trees. Then come the blue-ridge gorges before the Great Plateau.

Shimmer green, shimmer blue,
Staircase upon staircase
Rippling skywards
Through ancient time.

"Leon Garcia—at your service." Solid handshake, smile like Valentino's, insisting on conversing in English. "I am to instruct you every bit I know, very well?" It had been a year since Doctor Garcia had seen his wife and two children, back in Havana; exactly the same time since Malenga had seen her father Julius. "But first you tell life story, a bargain?"

Afterwards she had asked, "Is Angola such a wonderful cause that you leave your family thousands of miles away?"

"One day there will be the real peace, not this pretending. And Angola will grow big in love. Then for certain I bring my family . . . You see, here I am needed. There is great joy in being needed."

What Garcia said next would have to be his epitaph: "Thus I belong."

To be needed, and to belong—ah yes, Malenga Nakale understands such sentiments. Otherwise, why is she here?

Garcia had designed the Medical Centre, the first of its kind in the bush. With the assistance of the villagers, he had cleared the ground, constructed it. With the equipment supplied by friendly nations, he had fitted it out.

At the opening ceremony there was dancing and singing, a games tournament, a visit from a FAPLA general who read a telegram of congratulation from the President of the Republic. "Malenga, you and me, we make history!"

"Smell it, Sparkler—the water?"

Musso: "Sparkler can only smell himself, Boss."

Noon, the air is cooler here beside the river. "Kip

stations!" Zorro pulls Malenga towards a sturdy sapling, sits her down, brings her arms back around the trunk, handcuffs her wrists. "Taking no chances, Sheba. You're worth your weight in uranium."

So this is what it means to be needed.

Knees up: hard cushions, but tumbling into a profound sleep. Only in her awakening do the memories return: the explosion, Dédo's screaming, the severed foot, the anguish of Salu, the terror in the eyes of the women.

Cardinal is tipping her head back, offering her water. "A word of warning, Miss Nakale." His politeness is almost comical. "Boss is on the bottle. That means he's . . . well, his temper's quicker to boil than usual. Don't provoke him."

"Thanks for the warning."

"Biscuit?—they're almond-flavoured." He snaps the biscuit into small pieces, feeds her. "And another thing—don't deny your name. It's the only thing that'll keep you alive."

Nose: beware of the bandit who offers kindness.

I wonder. She swallows. "Sergeant? You were the only one who didn't fire at Tomas."

"Tomas? Oh, the boy . . . There've been too many kids." He gets up. "In nineteen days, I'm out of his lot for good."

"Cardinal?" Zorro's voice comes sing-songing through the silence. He corks his bottle. He unhooks his earphones. "Stop soft-soaping, Soldier. Prisoners get round your little finger, remember."

Cardinal offers no defence. He removes himself, lies against a tree.

"What's the bloody Queen of Sheba want, Cardinal?"

Cardinal has closed his eyes. "She was asking . . ."

"Asking what?"

"If it ever rains."

Chapter Three

To ward off sleep, Tomas shakes his head, presses it against the cool barrel of his hunting gun, retrieved from among the reeds at the river bank. He takes a swig from his water bottle. Old Maria will have arranged for the dead to be buried, and she will have sent to FAPLA for help.

Tomas perceives only one duty in this world, to keep his adopted sister in sight.

I, Tomas, swear to Choko the Wise; Tomas of the Nine Lives—Maradona! Garcia had said of him, "Drop this kid by parachute anywhere in Angola and he wing it back quicker than homing pigeon."

Four soldiers, and I have three bullets only. Also, he is mindful of Malenga's Great Rule: killing a human can never be justified.

"Never, Sister?"

"No, never . . . You can think it sometimes, but never do it."

"I do not understand. The animals of the forest know —that you have to kill."

"The animals must kill to survive. That is not so with humans. They have the choice."

Tomas dimly remembers his mother and his father. They had no choice. Sometimes I think she is my kid sister. She understands so little.

Suddenly he is alert, disturbed by the voice of the fat soldier calling to his captain. "Boss—Boss!" Musso is pointing across the river. "Something out there!"

The White Wolves spring to defensive stations behind the trees, AK-47s steadied, aimed. Driftwood?

There is the palest glaze on the water.

"Definitely, Boss."

Nothing definite, nothing at all.

Cardinal has taken out his binoculars. He focuses them, rescues Musso from a verbal roasting which Zorro is on the point of administering. "He's right, Boss."

"Let's see."

"Dinghy . . . One leg over the side."

Zorro registers amazement. "That's South African issue—this far?"

Obstructed only momentarily, the dinghy shifts in the current, leaves behind entanglement and shadow, enters the light.

"One body . . . It's a wonder the crocs haven't had him for brekkers. Mussolini?"

"Boss?"

"Sniff, sniff—go fetch!"

"Can't swim, Boss."

Cardinal can: up to his chest, then dog-paddling, meeting the dinghy halfway across the river.

Zorro: "That leg over the side, comrades, is uniform. One of ours."

Malenga has been visited by ants, giant ones. This must be their tree, their kingdom. She struggles up, shaking ants from her shoe. They're trapped in the laces.

"Stay still, Sheba!"

She hates the creatures, stamps on them. "Off!"

Sparkler has joined Cardinal waist-high in the river. They are bringing a body ashore.

"A chicken, Boss—pure chicken."

A young soldier; South African. "A call-up bleeding Charlie!"

"Ants!"

"Shut up, Sheba!"

"Ripped off his badges, Boss."

"A frigging deserter!"

The youth is lowered on to dried mud.

"Still ticking, then, Cardinal?"

"Just about."

"Wake up, Sonny Jim!"

"See, Boss, he got one in the hand." Musso indicates the youth's crudely bandaged left wrist and palm. "Shot while escaping, I reckon."

Zorro concedes, "At least the jerk remembered his training." The youth has plastered his face, neck, throat and arms with mud as protection against the heat. Only his rimless spectacles permit a glimpse of the human beneath the mask.

Cardinal has examined the young soldier's pockets. "Chucked his papers away, of course."

"Drill the yellow rat, Boss!"

Zorro scoops river water over the youth's face. "Let's see what colour he is." Mud retreats, sunlight advances, on ginger hair. "Unless they're producing Zulus with carrot rinses these days, this is one of the brethren."

"He's no brethren of mine," protests Musso. As if fearing his commander might neglect his duty, the fat man adds, "A ruddy deserter, Boss."

The ants are biting. Malenga had resolved, 'Beg no favours of these killers'. Resolution succumbs to termites. "Please!"

The prisoner has been brought under the trees, close to Malenga. "Let me treat him. I'm a nurse, remember."

"And you're Malenga Nakale, right?"

"Yes," she admits. "What's left of me."

Zorro releases her. She stoops, beats away the ants.

"Rightee, Sheba, you can earn your keep. I want Four-Eyes Ginger-Nut here to have a wash and brush up and be ready to march, *molto presto, comprende*?"

Sparkler is unhappy. "That boy bad luck, Boss. River not like you steal what belong to it."

"This zombie belongie to White Wolves, Chummy, not the Ovimbundu."

"But river belong Ovimbundu, Boss."

"Wrong again. This is socialist Angola, are you forgetting? River belong everybody."

"Not when Big Man rule," persists Sparkler. "Then only Ovimbundu own river."

"A week after your Chief Cockerel takes over this waterway, my friends, it'll be dyed his favourite colour." Zorro remembers the poet among them. He stares at Malenga. "Blood River."

She washes the youth with water brought from the river by Sparkler. She examines him as best she can. He is about her age, her height. For such a slim frame, he has big feet; protruding knees.

Gangly.

I can imagine the fun they make of him. It's written all over him: No Good at Sport. Trips over things.

"You can spot them a mile away," Zorro is saying. "The fairies."

Acute exhaustion, she decides.

Cardinal: "Kids—we shouldn't be calling up kids."

"War did my kid brother no harm," counters Zorro. "He turned out a hero. OK, he's a dead hero—"

"Water!" interrupts Malenga. "To drink."

"Give her yours, Fat Man, and don't whine on about 'Why me, Boss?'"

Malenga unstoppers the flask. Without looking round, she puts the water to her own lips and drinks.

"Boss, she—"

"Shut up, Mussolini. She tricked you. She's brains. Already working out how she can give us the slip. You shouldn't have refused her her ration back there."

"Me, Sir?—it was you, Boss."

"I didn't hear that insubordinate remark, Fat Man."

Rash when provoked, Musso knows how to irritate. "She'll have you on a string, Boss, if you're not careful."

The prisoner's head rests on her arm. She eases open his mouth, presses down the tongue gently, administers life-restoring fluid.

Nothing seems broken. The left hand is the only injury Malenga can find. It is tied with a piece of shirting. It stinks of new mud dried over old mud. The fingers are white, dusty with congealed blood.

She undoes the bandage. It sticks to flesh.

The White Wolves relish the extra rest. A can of beer passes from hand to hand. Zorro lets Musso have first swig. It settles his temper.

"I was thinking, Boss, when the Big Man and UNITA take over, they'll make Sparkler here Minister for Rehabilitation."

Zorro appreciates the joke. "I like it. There you go, Sparkler—promotion. Remember all the bridges we've taken out, all the kimbos, the factories, the power stations, not to mention the oil terminal?—well it'll be your job to rebuild 'em."

Sparkler isn't certain how to respond to this vision of his future. "Sure, Boss."

"And you know what'll happen then? Us Whiteys'll come back and blow 'em all up again."

A poem is forming: about this modern Moses cradled in the bulrushes. I'm not sure who's worse off, soldier, you or me.

"Is he breathing, Sheba?"

"Yes, but he needs rest."

"He walks. Or we deliver him back into the arms of Ol' Man River."

Moses, lifeless lies
Front towards the enemy.

She has poured surgical spirit on to a swab. The stinging touch makes the youth jerk back his hand.

"Sorry."

His eyes flicker open, widen at the sight of her.

"It's got to be cleaned." Dirt and blood cover the swab. "A couple of times more . . . no, don't close the palm."

Sparkler has become restless with waiting. "Why you want boy march with us, Boss, if quick knife solve problem?"

"Because of something you Zulus can't comprehend, Sparkler—justice. We shall protect this kid with our lives. We shall try him, find him guilty of desertion and shoot him. That's justice!"

The deserter is looking up at her. He's got freckles. It almost makes her laugh: to be in all this trouble, and to have freckles too. "He's a long way from home," she hears herself say.

"I think she fancies him, Boss."

Cardinal seems to approve. "Babes in the wood."

Malenga applies clean bandaging to the wounded hand, then deals with the young man's glasses, wiping off the grime of dead flies. His eyes search her face—for comfort, for trust?

"There." She replaces the glasses. "Now you can see what a wonderful world it is."

Handcuffed, prisoner to prisoner, two-abreast in the bush. Barbs of branches, claws, dripping syrup that stings.

Tomas, are you out there, little brother?

Steel chafing against skin. Hear the rattle. No words, but a sudden holding of hands—the only way. Wiry fingers. Keep the elbows in, watch the steps ahead.

Bumping. "How're you feeling?"

"Terrible."

At least the sun's gone.

"I'm Malenga."

"Hamish. Nice to meet you!"

"They kidnapped me."

"For your bedside manner?"

"They liked the sound of my name."

"Yes, it's very musical." Hamish thanks her for helping him. "If it hadn't been for you, they'd have left me."

"My pleasure—but you got me off the hook too."

"It was nothing—movies are my thing."

They are referring to a small triumph of prisoner over captor. As Zorro had clipped the handcuffs on the wrists of Malenga and Hamish, he had said, "OK, I'm offering the last can of beer to any of you who knows in which movie the hero and the heroine spent the night together, handcuffed."

Musso had groaned, his face tumbling—"spare us another film quiz, Boss."

Sparkler had covered his face, pretending to think. Cardinal had shaken his head.

"Guess, Cardinal."

"Nothing comes to mind, Boss."

"Guess, man!"

"Baby Face Nelson?"

"Wrong. You owe me half a day's pay . . . Well, Sheba, you're the educated one around her. Handcuffs. A honey blonde. An English upper crust gent with marbles in his mouth. Try."

"I'm sorry, I—"

"Think, or are you too stuck up for films? Prefer opera, do you, Sheba?" He had pushed her as if her inability to answer was a deliberate insult. He screamed, "Think!"

The answer came, not from Malenga but from the young deserter:

"The Thirty-Nine Steps."

No gratitude. Zorro rounded on the prisoner. "I didn't ask you, boy. Traitors are disqualified."

Cardinal showed his impatience. "Captain, let's get moving."

"Wait." The barrel of Zorro's AK-47 had swung up under the deserter's chin. "Let us up the odds, shall we? *The Thirty-Nine Steps* it is. Now I want you to tell me who directed the film, and when, or you're a dead man."

"Captain!"

"Shut up, Sergeant."

Malenga remembered the flash of sunlight on the prisoner's glasses and on the gun barrel at his throat.

"Director and year, Mister Wise Guy."

The future was on Cardinal's face as he watched the scene with resigned horror. Yes, men have died this way, his expression seemed to indicate: believe it.

"Proceed, Boy!"

Malenga: "You can't expect him—" She is silenced by a blow from the back of Zorro's hand.

"I'm waiting."

"The Thirty-Nine Steps—"

"We have already ascertained the title, Dickhead . . . Director and date or you're vulture-meat."

Hamish protested about the gun in his throat. "I can't answer if you choke me." Small point won: steel no longer squashes Adam's apple. "Right." He blew out air, tightened his jaw. "Now, what was the question again?"

In any other circumstance, Malenga would have laughed. He was playing with Zorro; playing with fire.

"How many guesses do I have?"

"One. And before I count up to five."

"Only five?"

"Counting, Carrot-brain: one . . . and two . . . and three . . ."

"Well—"

"And four . . ."

"Alfred Hitchcock directed."

"Date, before five—one, and two, and—"

"Made in 1936. It was remade in 1959 with Kenneth Moore and later with Robert Powell—"

"Enough!"

"It starred Robert Donat and Madeleine Carroll—"

"Stop!"

"With Lucie Mannheim, Peggy Ashcroft and Wylie Watson." The youth's next words appeared to crush Zorro the

Film Buff. "Everybody knows that, Captain." He had held out his hand for the prize. It was not forthcoming.

His word had stunned the White Wolves:

"Cheat."

And nothing happened. Zorro merely stared at the prisoner. He ripped open the can of beer. He emptied it over Hamish's feet.

"I'll take your word for it, son. But I don't remember Peggy Ashcroft being in *The Thirty Nine Steps*."

"You pushed your luck," Malenga is saying.

"He annoyed me. It's against regulations to shove loaded guns into people."

Like the darkness before dawn, the forest has thickened before the ascent to the plateau. The White Wolves breach the way ahead with machetes.

"Keep close." Zorro chops and talks. He has opened the Book of Hamish. "This prisoner of ours, gentlemen, sure knows his movies." He hacks, sweeps aside every obstruction. "And what does that tell us about him? . . . Musso, you're a student of human nature."

Musso curses. His arms are a battlefield of blood and sweat. "A wasted youth, Boss."

"Precisely. I predict that when the interrogations get under way . . ." A snake uncoils from the tree branch above him. He cuts it in half. "We'll discover he is uneducated, unqualified—your poor pathetic white, neglected by semi-literate parents . . . And probably a dreamer."

Zorro halts, peers around him. "Just like me!"

Malenga asks her partner, "Is he right?"

Hamish returns a lopsided grin. "And some natural history."

Zorro's voice sing-songs above the sounds of the machetes. "Attached to this white trash is your . . . educated Black. She's got GCSEs from an English public school. It's written all over her . . . And while he's chicken-shit—less than nothing, she's the daughter of the most wanted man in Africa.

"What a movie *that'd* make!"

Musso: "Pity it'll all end in tears, Boss."

The route opens, the march accelerates.

"Hamish sounds Scottish."

"My Dad's side."

"You wouldn't be Hamish of Hamish and the Golden Fish, would you?"

"The what?"

"A fairy story. Hamish was a boy who saved the life of a golden fish. But it's a sad tale because the three wishes the fish promised him never came true."

"Just my luck, even in stories. Funny, my Dad never told me that one. He taught me the fife, though. Couldn't afford bagpipes. And he got me reading Walter Scott."

"And your mother?"

"Portuguese originally."

"Then you speak Tuga?"

"Sort of . . . You British?"

"Angolan."

He laughs. "Me too, if they'll have me."

"What made you—?"

"Decide to desert? I didn't. I escaped. Out of that lot for good."

"On your own?"

Is it the dusk which has drawn the warmth from Hamish's

face? Or a dark secret? "The less you know about me, Malenga, the better."

"You think I'll split on you?"

"Not willingly." He pauses. He will not tell her anything more for the present. "You don't know how these maniacs operate."

Darkness; marching at a quicker pace, cold air as difficult to breathe in as hot air. One stop only, for half an hour, yet enough time to descend into a turmoil of sleep. Then dawn, Musso the alarm clock, using his boot to wake the prisoners. He curses them, and he curses the blistering return of the eternal sun.

Pins and needles, neck-stiff, back-stiff, cramp in the legs; feeling horrible. How easy it would be to say, "I resign —shoot me".

Heat swells up from the earth, pulsing between the trees. The air crackles with insects.

"March!"

"Where?"

"Somewhere over the rainbow."

Above, a white-blazing sky presses heat upon heat. Sweat in the eyes, in trickles down stomach and spine, in torrents from armpits; feet-squelching, chin-dripping. Ankles sore with rubbing.

Chained

We feed together
Sweat together
Wet together
Bleed together
Think together

Stink together
Could this be love?

The forest is thinning as the track rises to higher ground. Suddenly, ahead, streams slice ravines of deep-sea blue soaring into emerald; and the wind is the breath of the savannah.

"What's beyond the bushland, children?"

A forest of hands: "me, Miss!"

"Let somebody else have a turn, Tomas . . . Dédo?"

"The High Plateau, Miss."

At last air you can breathe without it toasting your insides. This light is a dream.

The White Wolves also celebrate the land open to the sky. Zorro's "Take twenty" is drowned by cries of "Water!"

Cascading, bouncing, crashing, streaking the yellow-ochre rocks with silver and rainbows.

"Come on, Malenga!" Hand-grasping, tugging, young fawn leaping. Under the waterfall. "Yah!" Both, gulping down more than any medical book would recommend. "Who cares about belly-ache?"

For a boy under sentence of death, this prisoner is mighty cheerful: has he forgotten?

"I could eat worms, Malenga."

She shakes her head and water jets out into the dazzling air. "You'd have to keep them two days at least." She senses him look at her with admiration: mud gone, sweat gone.

"Why, Doctor?"

"In case the worms'd eaten poisonous plants."

"They say you're FAPLA-trained, is that true?"

"Nothing they say is true."

Hamish follows his own thoughts. "In the jungle, my pal

Dirk and me ate wild rhubarb . . . was that right, eating rhubarb?"

"So long as you didn't chew the leaves."

Garcia, they couldn't kill the voice that lives in me, what you taught me. Plants with milky sap?—avoid them. Anything coloured red?—leave it well alone. And beware fruits that divide into five segments.

"Dirk didn't have the strength to chew."

"I thought you said, the less I know about you, the better."

There is no time for a reply. Zorro stands above them, against the shimmering afternoon. "Seen this, Gendarmes? They're bloody lovers already."

All eyes. "You should never've put 'em in handcuffs, Boss."

"I'm planning the future, Fat Man—Africa's future: bringing Black and White together in harmony."

As it is intended to, the comment stirs mirth among the White Wolves. Even Cardinal smiles. Zorro appreciates this from him. "That right, Cardinal?"

"It's what we pray for, Boss."

"And what we fight for. Clear out the Reds, then let the Whites and the Blacks live in peace . . . Under our say-so, correct?"

Musso proposes, "We ought to marry 'em, Boss."

"Sure, then we shoot 'em for illegal cohabitation."

Laughter ricochets down the valley.

Chapter Four

The eye is dazzled by surfaces that are no longer earth but satin—burnished, teased into folds of purple, by a sky too spectacular for even poets to describe. Malenga stores away a human image in all this natural splendour: on the tabletop of the world, the shadow of prisoners chained together.

Nothing makes sense.

"If you reckon this is beautiful," says Hamish, "then you'd think sunset over the Okavango was a miracle."

Miracles are in short supply. "You've been there?"

"I've been nowhere. Except in my head. But one day I will."

Malenga tells Hamish that somewhere north of here she had her first posting—Malanje, beside another river, the Lucala. She'd written a poem about the Lucala. The script of it is a pile of ash in the entrails of the Medical Centre.

Hamish asks, "Why does Zorro say your Dad's the most wanted man in Africa? Is he a terrorist?"

A smile. "Julius would prefer to be called a politician."

"Is he rich? I mean, that's why they've kidnapped you, isn't it?"

"It's not Dad's money they want."

Hamish nods. He has seen enough films, with scenes of kidnap and abduction, to get the message. "That means we've both got to make a run for it. And soon."

Close your eyes and just jump? In this heat, without food or water, unprotected in the craft of survival?

Suicide.

"After all, I did it once."

"And the crocodiles were about to have you for elevenses."

"But two of us!" His mind dances with plans, with fear and with hope. "Look, who's this Big Man they're all scared to death of, the Chief Cockerel, and why's Zorro got this joke about you two enjoying each other's company?"

"The Big Man is the monster in every Angolan's dream . . . only when people wake up, he's still there, him and his bandits, massacring whole villages—with South African guns, South African rockets . . . And blowing them up with South African mines."

Dédo, remember me?

"Not Robin Hood, then?"

"Is that how the Boers think of him?"

"I read he went down big in the States . . . Because he kills commies, is it?" His thoughts switch again to escape. "Don't you trust me, Malenga?"

"Trust you?"

"We've got to give them the slip, before we reach the Big Man's camp. Still, you hate South Africans, so why should you want my company?"

Malenga senses he is baiting a trap and decides not to be tempted. "I can tell the difference between people and persons."

"Yet you can't forget my colour?"

"*Your* colour? That should be my line, shouldn't it?"

He is sore. "You're a hard nut, Malenga Nakale."

"And you like feeling sorry for yourself." It is an unkind remark, and unfair.

OK, Mrs Trench, you put it in my school report, so I'll never forget: "Malenga always insists on having the last word."

Insists; that hurt.

"I'm sorry, Hamish. I'm so tired."

He beams. "Don't mention it. My Gran once said that sorry and thank you are the easiest things in the world to say—but the least said."

They walk through the night, taking few rests. To keep themselves awake, Hamish suggests, "I'll tell you something about me, then you tell me something about you. That way we'll grow to trust one another. It might be our last chance."

Malenga hears of Hamish's escape, with Dirk, two years his senior. "It was mostly Dirk's idea, escaping. He was the one with the brains. Him and me, we were a weird couple. He'd a university degree—a philosopher!—while I was a grocer's assistant. 'You ought to go to College,' he'd say. 'Study film, seeing you're so crazy about the movies.' Me—study!

"'You're an uncut diamond,' he said. 'Take it from me.' Nicest thing anybody ever said to me. It bucked me up, especially as at that time the Corporal was calling me Heap O'Shit and Sheep's Brain.

"These Namibian freedom fighters had come out of the bush thinking there was a truce. They got mowed down like grass. Our job, Dirk and me, was to bury them. That decided it for us. He was a long distance runner, and according to the Captain I'd a yellow streak as long as a croc's tail.

"We made good progress at first, but in the dark everything's confusing. I reckon we started going round in a circle. Anyway, we were spotted. Chased. Shot at. And Dirk got one in the back. There'd have been a second but for me catching this one." Hamish holds up his wounded hand. "Hurt worse than a cricket ball from one of your West Indian quickies.

"Dirk was finished. I knew that. I carried him. Strange, him being so rich, living on a farm stretching over hundreds of acres, yet thin as a rake.

"He'd been a great friend, though. Taught me a lot while we did training. Like it's OK for a man to enjoy poetry. Does that seem odd to you, Malenga?"

She shakes her head. "My own father thinks poetry's a luxury."

"Three days he hung on. Kept pleading with me to finish him off—we'd still got one rifle, to use for hunting. He was religious. If I shot him, then topped myself, we could go on being comrades in the next life.

"Some philosopher! I told him, 'We've things to do in this life. Like you buying me that ice-cream you promised, in Lubango, where the bushes are all scarlet with blossoms, or like me paddling you down to Okavango to photograph reed cormorants, black-winged stilts and lily-trotters'."

"Lily-trotters?"

"Yes, jacana—they've got great flat feet. You find them in the lily lagoons . . . Anyway, I woke up the fourth morning with another burying job on my hands. God, I wept. As much for myself as him, I suppose. Feeling sorry for myself, you see.

"The rest's history, as they say. But I'd one slice of luck. A lorry stopped for me. The driver was a Filipino, working for the Angolan government. He risked his life every day ferrying cargo from Lobito to the south. UNITA had caught him twice. He'd escaped, second time minus one eye . . . but it didn't stop him doing his bit for the Republic. I thought, good on ye—so far from home."

"Like my Dr Garcia."

"Like you too, Malenga . . . Afterwards, I got very lost, then very ill. I planned to die by the river. And then I saw this dinghy stuck in the bushes. It'd been there since the last invasion.

"I must have slept for a week on that luxury cruise . . . Huh, the story of my life—out of the frying pan and into the fire."

"Talking of fire . . ." It is Malenga's turn to relieve the tedium of the journey. "We used to live in this ground-floor flat in London—Tufnell Park on the lousy Northern Line. Most of the time there was just Fransina and me, while Julius shuttled between Harare and New York, working to get Mandela released.

"We were followed everywhere. By South African secret police. Whatever we did, we were watched. Once they tried to bundle my mother into a car. Threatening phone calls several times a week—they were normal; but on this occasion somebody chucked a petrol bomb through the front room window. The place blew up!"

"With you inside?"

"That was *our* lucky break. No, Fransina and me were in the yard at the back. It was summer and we'd been sitting out there, yammering. A wind blew the door to, and we were locked out!

"Within a week I was packed off to a boarding school in the Malvern Hills, where they taught me to become an English Lady."

"Sounds painful."

"All-girls schools usually are."

Hamish's turn and he tells Malenga of his dream, "To explore the length and breadth of this great continent, on foot and by canoe—dinghies are definitely out. I've achieved nothing, you see. I couldn't write till I was eight and my Ma was still tying my shoelaces when I got into double-figures . . . But I'll show her. If it takes me twenty years, I'll do something in this life that'll make her proud of me."

"Isn't she now—proud of you?"

"A bit, maybe."

"I guess what you really want is to be proud of yourself."

He bows his head. "I haven't made a particularly good start, have I—a deserter?"

Malenga is not prepared to let him feel sorry for himself again.

"If it makes any difference, *I'm* proud of you. For what you did."

"Truly?"

"Cross my heart and hope to die." She shivers, then chuckles. "Though in the circumstances, that's not the best way of putting it."

"Thanks all the same."

Day: tides of hot air fire-flick the landscape, melting it. Silent now, too exhausted to speak, stumbling, head afloat, skin sweat-sore, salt dried in cracks, lips swollen.

"Soon," predicts Zorro as afternoon wheels, white-hot towards evening. Ahead, a forest of mopanes, called butterfly trees, seemingly lifted from the earth and suspended over a seething void.

"OK, Sparkler—your tribe. Tiptoe through the tulips and tell them to roll out the red carpet."

"Red carpet, Boss?"

"Just warn them I don't want any trigger-happy coolies cutting short my manhood."

The pennant Sparkler ties to his AK-47 displays the black eland, emblem of UNITA.

"You have my permission to begin shaking in your shoes, Sheba."

No need to be warned. UNITA spells death in twenty different ways, all horrific. Those they don't shoot, they dismember with axes, knives, machetes—to save on bullets. And when it suits them, they burn people alive.

Malenga has seen the photographs. What's the word the Republican government uses to describe members of UNITA, dead or alive?—*elements*. Very appropriate. Not men, not persons, not individuals—but elements.

A broad, sandy track splits the mopane woods. In the gloom, Malenga makes out gates, barbed wire, turrets of sandbags. Closer, she discerns gun emplacements, Panhard armoured vehicles between the trees. Beneath her feet the ground bears the recent imprint of tracked weaponry.

They approach the Free Capital of Angola, a title awarded it by Zorro without conviction.

"Halt!" Elements of UNITA fan out in front of the White Wolves.

Hamish: "No sign of that red carpet."

"Shut up, Squeamish!"

Zorro addresses the sentries. "It's all right, kiddos, we're kosher. We OK, heap big heroes—tell the imbecile, Sparkler."

Boss seems not to have been recognized. The realization offends him. He talks over Sparkler's translation. "Captain Hargreaves of Koevoet, who're the bleeding saviours of your necks, boyos."

Malenga is told to empty out the contents of her medical case. At first she wants to spread a cover over the dirt track. "Medical instruments, they've got to be kept—"

"Tip it out, Bitch!"

"Do exactly as the man says, Sheba." Is even Zorro afraid?

Out come supplies, fresh, good quality—a gift of the Italian people to the Republic of Angola: the codeine, the antibiotics, the immodium Malenga has treated Sparkler with, though it had scarcely influenced his diarrhoea; the antihistamine—what's left of it after treating the White Wolves for mosquito bites; the water sterilisation tablets, plasters; and finally, curiously, a postcard of an old Portuguese candy floss seller in Lubango, which she'd intended to give to Dédo.

"We'll have those," orders Zorro, picking up a packet of surgical blades. "Just in case the prisoner goes for her own throat before we can swap her for a queen's ransom."

"Or the Big Man's throat."

"Don't go putting ideas into her head, Cardinal."

Zorro and his men are being treated coolly. He does not understand this. Such an indifferent reception conflicts with the image he has portrayed of himself, as one of the stars in the Big Man's heaven. Always his theme has been—they owe us everything.

He is to be further insulted. The White Wolves are ordered to hand in their arms. The incredulous silence obliges the duty corporal to repeat, "No guns!"

"Something's up, Boss."

Zorro burns. "What movie are we supposed to have landed in, Toadface, eh—your spaghetti western where the cowpokes've to strip off their hardware before they're allowed in the saloon?"

The UNITA corporal understands not a word of Zorro's tirade. "Knives too."

Cardinal also protests. "We're allies," he says, "It's wrong."

"Allies? Koevoet, allies with this Black rabble?—do me a favour!" Zorro burns, Zorro blazes. "Masters! . . . Listen—we call the tune around here. We train you, we arm you, we fund you, we dig you out of the shit."

Cardinal has struggled to contain his own anger. He tries to soothe that of his commander. "Forget it, Boss. It's natural: we help them, they hate us."

Zorro is not so easily pacified. "We're away ten days, Comrades. We cut Angolan throats on their behalf, blow Angolan bridges, cause mayhem to all and sundry. Who for?—for the biggest jerk in Africa. We return home with a hot property—and this is his thanks." He turns. "I smell a rat, lads. One rat in particular—the Yankee peacemaker's in town. Is Maynard up your nose too, Fat Man?"

"There's a stench coming from somewhere, Boss."

Through the camp gates Malenga sees bodies, heaps of them awaiting transport; to be dumped in the bush.

Zorro is offended. "Why don't you clean up your rubbish?"

"Still twitching, Boss. Ruddy disgusting!"

Malenga feels Hamish's fist tight round hers: it's a comfort.

There are women among the dead, all of them young.

Malenga is recalling her father's words: "Poetry, Malenga? Oh no. That's for people who sit at home and dream of daffodils. What the world wants is men and women of action. That's the only poetry which means anything—the poetry of action."

OK, Julius, so I took action. Here I am. Is this what you'd want for me?

Unfair. Julius and Fransina broke a gut as well as the bank to shield me from the consequences of their lives. Then what made me break cover?

Goodbye, Daffs.

I'm thinking of your favourite word, Julius—*destiny*. Ah yes, well just about now destiny's going to walk right over me.

They pass stockpiles of ammunition, armoured trucks, jeeps, artillery placed haphazardly among the mopanes. A second barricade of sandbag walls and barbed wire guards the entrance to the Big Man's kingdom—once a Protestant mission, surrounded by wattle-and-clay huts with thatched roofs.

It has been expanded to accommodate scores of troops. For the other ranks there are frame tents, ex-American army issue; for the officers, cabins prefabricated in Johannesburg.

Between two mopanes a huge banner offers, in English, a welcome to visitors:

YOU ARE ENTERING FREE ANGOLA

And printed below, in smaller letters:

GOD IN HEAVEN, THE BIG MAN ON EARTH

Zorro comments on the new uniforms, new weapons. "Santa Claus will have delivered some very cosy missiles too, I guess. You see, Sheba, hereabouts we get the Black man to fight for apartheid."

There is to be a more respectful greeting for the White

Wolves from a young officer called Roberto, who received his training from Zorro. He salutes smartly, addresses Zorro in a kind of English. "Us much pleasured to view you bleeding return OK, Sir."

"My God, Cardinal, Robbo's gone from corporal to lieutenant in under a fortnight."

"FAPLA hit us much bleeding bad, Sir." Glancing at Malenga, Roberto says, "Miss Nakale, I presume."

"Ours!" snaps Zorro.

"The Chief, he demand bleeding see her."

Zorro knows he has no choice. "So long Big Chief remember notice round bleeding neck, Robbo—'Keep off bleeding grass' . . . And this stiff—" he points at Hamish "—is ours too. Stick him in the Sin Bin till we decide if he's worth keeping warm."

Hamish is telling Malenga, "Don't worry, I'll think of something." It's as funny as his freckles: what, sprout wings, head for the Okavango Delta on a beam of light?

She feels the wrench. He has become her friend. The cuffs slip from her wrist.

He had packed her medical case for her, carried it. Now he hands it back to her. "Okavango—don't forget!"

Malenga suddenly wants him to know her feelings. She grasps his arm. Awkwardly, she holds it towards Zorro. "This hand will need a new dressing."

"Take him," commands Zorro, "before I wet myself."

Chapter Five

Lieutenant Roberto delivers his orders: "You make mighty clean wash-up, Miss Nakale. And enrobe proper bleeding smart ass. Big Man grant you great prejudice."

Malenga laughs, answers him in Tuga. "Privilege, do you mean?"

Relieved to be able to speak in his own language, Roberto says Captain Hargreaves taught him his English. "He tells me the wrong words for things—then I make a fool of myself. They all laugh . . . Now hurry, please."

The London Hilton can have nothing on this shower-bath among the mopanes: chain to bucket, bucket tilting on wooden axis, and the water strikes the most welcome blow any prisoner could pray for; only the luxury of the moment is spoilt by the gawpers.

Roberto has offered Malenga fruit and South African canned beer. I ought to reject the beer, on principle. She opens it. Sorry Fransina, hope you'll understand—needs must. She drinks. She asks, "Could you get some of this to my friend?"

"You claim to be Angolan, right?" answers Roberto. "Then how can you call a South African your friend?"

"I might say the same for you—aren't the South Africans your friends?"

"Never," replies Roberto vehemently. "They are allies of UNITÁ, but not our friends."

"If we are both Angolans, why are we fighting one another?"

"I fight for free Angola. Against one-party state."

"Is killing your own people the way to bring about freedom and democracy?"

Roberto closes the debate with a grin. "You're a Nakale through and through, Miss." He shrugs, stares past her towards the north. "I gave up trying to understand things long ago. Out there's my family. If I don't fight, I'll be killed—*they'll* be killed."

"The Government's offered an amnesty to all UNITA."

"They would only come after me. Send the evil spirits."

"Roberto, men don't need ghostly spirits to make them evil."

In the prison compound, Hamish Ross holds tight to a dream: the Okavango; and he is drifting free under the stars with Malenga.

Ma'll get a shock at first, but she'll come to like Malenga eventually, as I do. Trouble is, I'm not good enough for her. If circumstances were different—if we were free to choose our own company—she'd not touch me with a cattle prod.

Feet lodged in forked branches, hidden among the mopanes, is Tomas of the Nine Lives. This evening he speared a rabbit, skinned it, ate it raw. He is short of water—and of sleep.

A trumpet-blast cuts short his dozing. He climbs to a higher vantage point which offers him a view of the drill square. Troops are gathering from all sides. A small army of them, they squat down facing in one direction.

"Movies!"

Roped across two mopanes is a screen of cotton fabric which has been unrolled from a long wooden pole.

"Movies, Boss!"

"Thank God it's not another six-hour speech." Zorro has insisted on the White Wolves escorting the prisoner, Nakale. "We're not letting her out of our sight, Robbo."

"What film do you reckon it'll be, Boss—*King Kong*?"

Zorro cannot conceal a rush of boyish delight. "Movies under the stars—nothing like it!" He commends Musso for his perceptiveness. "Kong went to America, but he didn't get the Stars and Stripes treatment, did he?"

"Not like Big Man Kong did, Boss."

The last of the twilight has drained from the butterfly woods. Choirs of crickets resist the encroaching silence. Through the darkest glades, bats flit with urgent daring.

As for the humans present, they sit in dirt, save for one, a figure at the centre of the front row of the stalls. The Chief Cockerel is clad in crisp-pressed combat trousers, with the stars of a general on his epaulettes and a death's-head symbol on his beret; the only person to be permitted a chair.

Beside him, crouching or kneeling, are the Big Man's senior staff. Then, in obedient rows sit the world's most expensively equipped rebel troops, from colonels and captains to corporals and raw squaddies, most of them Tomas's age.

Malenga has seen the harvest of this man's war, his thirst for power which no amount of innocent blood can quench. She feels disgust. Everything is surfacing, a turmoil of feelings, dominated by anger, threatening to crush the voice of caution which says, 'If you wish to survive, be silent, accept.'

Accept? Never.

Cardinal has been watching her. "Easy," he says.

A high-backed truck with South African markings is mounted with a 35-mm film projector working off a small but noisy generator. The projectionist is identified by Zorro. "I thought our Yankee sweatbag would be behind this. There's your prize mischief-maker, Sheba. Cecil B. De Mille, alias Henry Maynard, Mister Central Intelligence Agency, here to stir the crap and smoke out commies across the length and breadth of the continent."

Malenga takes in the view of Henry Maynard—in his fifties, flabby, wearing braces over a sweat-stained shirt, dabbing feverishly at his forehead with an outsize rag.

The Big Man has raised his officer's baton, a silver-topped cane: action!

Through a loudhailer the American announces, in broken Portuguese, that the titling and introductory music of the film have yet to be added. "The movie is to be called *Angola—Destiny of a Nation*."

That word again: destiny.

Malenga listens to the cheers and the applause. She remembers something Zorro said: "We made peace in order to carry on the war."

If you do not want to watch, close your eyes; but is that enough? Yes, if you want to stay alive.

The film, declares Maynard, is to be in English, for it is aimed at western audiences. "People of the advanced nations must be persuaded there will never be genuine peace in this country till the so-called People's Republic ceases to be a satellite of the Soviets, and agrees to share power with the UNITA democrats. The nation's future must be free!"

Malenga watches the heroic saga of the Chief Cockerel and his followers; their dedication to the destiny of a nation. She sees documentary footage of a war that long ago passed its quarter-century: invasion by aircraft, invasion by tanks, by armoured vehicles smothering the bush in fire and smoke.

She sees villages taken, villagers slaughtered; factories, power stations, water purifiers gutted; oil terminals mined, harbours destroyed and—of course—bridges demolished.

Ours was only a little bridge.

Along every road and track, in every ditch, the camera trespasses upon the dead.

Destiny.

Words, Julius.

But that's the point, Child—words are everything.

Superimposed on the scenes of devastation are other images, of the face of the hero: the Big Man in Washington, Paris, London: the Big Man shaking hands with diplomats and company executives; appearing on television, receiving ovations for his speeches.

Destiny.

Words: it all depends on who defines them, doesn't it, Julius?

Of course. That is why we fight—to make our definitions the ones that count.

Do the dead have a say?

As the film's spectators are intended to, Malenga notes the Big Man's exquisitely tailored clothes. Ah yes, the Gucci Guerrilla. Fransina once said, "He loves to wear white gloves. He thinks they make him look like an emperor, when in fact you'd mistake him for a traffic cop."

Didn't the White Rabbit in *Alice's Adventures in Wonderland* wear white gloves?

On how many corpses
In how many streets
From Lobito to Mocadames,
From Pangala to Catola
(Remember Cassinga?)
Has the Gucci Guerrilla
Left his visiting card
Embossed with South African gold,
His white gloves stained
With his nation's blood?

Is there a truth in things? Malenga Nakale would like to know. Forget my mind, my blood is telling me all this is twisted truth. The night's cool: I'm seething. Got to keep control. Yet my temper is gelignite. I can't breathe.

The signs have been assembled to create one meaning: in all these scenes of carnage, the Big Man is innocent; he is protecting his followers from FAPLA, the butchers.

Who bombed this countryside factory and murdered its workers?—why, FAPLA, to make it look like the UNITA bandits had done it. Who laid the mines under soft earth and blew the limbs off these people gathered in queues outside this shell-damaged hospital?—why FAPLA, to make it look like wicked UNITA had done it.

Zorro has not left Malenga's side. He shrugs. He confesses, "OK, it's a bit over the top. But it's what you do with information these days."

Through the loudhailer Maynard explains that there will be martial music at this point. "Specially composed by one of our Hollywood greats."

And at this point UNITA, armed with South African guns, firing South African ammunition, backed up by South

African armoured cavalry, mop up a defenceless kimbo.

The fault lies with the government of the People's Republic—for not surrendering to the triumphant forces of UNITA; for daring to believe that it is possible to create a society based upon equality and justice.

"Boss?" observes Musso. "I think our young panther's hackles are beginning to rise."

Hackles? Look it up in your dictionary, Tomas.

Hackles are the hair
On a dog's neck.
They signal his rage
Before he attacks
With savage teeth.

Malenga listens to the Big Man's dream of Africa. A united Africa.

"Under your rule, Sir?"

"One step at a time. First we must defeat the socialist disease in Africa."

"But if the People's Republic succeeds?"

"How can it when we shed so much of its people's blood?"

"They have abolished tribalism."

"We shall restore it. In future people will know their place. Where they belong. They will be happy once more."

The panther in Malenga escapes. She trembles with something beyond anger, almost a fit. She can see herself. She warns herself, yet she can control none of herself.

Hands are stiff, fingers outstretched. She clamps them over her ears, rams shut her mouth. It is not enough. She has bitten her tongue. She tastes the blood. She turns full round till her back faces the screen.

"What the . . . hell?" Zorro's exclamation punctures a

silence in the film's commentary. His words carry across the audience.

Cardinal foresees disaster. "Let her be, Boss. It'll soon be over." His message is ignored.

Zorro orders Malenga to remove her hands from her ears, to turn back to the screen. Molehill has become mountain. "Watch the film, Nakale!"

Malenga witnesses herself: the stupidity; yet she too ignores the message of caution.

It does not matter if I die.

She disobeys and is struck on the forearm. "Turn round, you Black scum!" For an instant it seems as if Zorro is issuing his command to the Big Man himself. "Goddam shift your ass!"

And the Big Man does shift his ass. He stands, signals for the film to be stopped.

"Oh my God!" mutters Cardinal.

Tomas, on his perch among the whispering butterfly leaves, also stands. He cradles his hunting gun between trunk and branch. He watches the troops of UNITA rise to their feet. They open a wide passage for the Big Man.

Guns bristle: quills of porcupine.

Malenga has protected her ears, her throat, but not her mouth. Zorro's fist comes down across her nose, her upper jaw. Her eyes fill, sting, she stumbles back.

Her arms are grasped. Zorro presents her to the saviour of Angola's people.

The Big Man has approached without haste. A few steps away from the captive, whose hands have been clamped to her side and not allowed to staunch the blood from her nose and mouth, he pauses.

"Give us the word, Chief, and we'll execute her immediately . . . Immediately!"

The Big Man has lifted a white-gloved hand as if about to conduct an orchestra. He is shorter than Malenga expected from his photographs, bulkier; older. There is grey in his beard. He lowers his ebony baton tipped with silver and his followers, as one man, sink to earth, eyes upturned.

They are used to speeches. The time has come for a speech.

Zorro presses Malenga to her knees. "You only need to give the order, Chief."

"In good time, Captain Hargreaves." This Zorro has no finesse. The Big Man waits; note, his silence seems to say, the contrast between the calm demeanour of a statesman and the crude temper of a Koevoet killer.

He speaks in perfect English. "Young lady, you choose to turn your back on our film—is that because of the truth it tells?"

He is Chief Cockerel now. There is wisdom in his gaze, worldly knowingness in the nod of his head. "Before us, Comrades," he says in Portuguese, "kneels a member of the Nakale family—infamous throughout the civilized world as terrorists.

"Her father Julius struts the stage of the United Nations, claiming to represent the oppressed black races of South Africa. But does he dare step on South African soil? Meanwhile his bombs destroy the innocent from Cape Town to Durban.

"Death to him!"

The Big Man beats the air with his baton and the UNITA freedom fighters who have destroyed the innocent from Quimbele to Xangongo give him answer:

"Death!"

"As for the prisoner's mother, she is in the pay of the so-called Angolan People's Republic. She sits in luxury in London and Paris, spewing out lies intended to besmirch the name of UNITA, to rouse ignorant liberals and lefties against our noble cause.

"Death to our enemies!"

"Death!"

"Comrades, we shall fight these people for ever. They are a disease, not only here in our beloved Angola, but now in Namibia. We shall destroy them here, and we shall destroy them in that country too."

"Death! Death! Death!" chant the faithful ranks of UNITA.

The Big Man lowers his voice, speaks to Malenga directly, in English once more. "What sort of fools are your parents to let you come here, where you can never belong?"

"They didn't let me come here, I—"

"Silence!" barks Zorro, hand around her neck, shaking her.

The Big Man has aroused his own passions with his speech. He is calm no longer. His finesse is shed. "The Nakales do nothing by accident, woman. They sent you to spy on us."

"No!" protests Malenga.

"Si-lence!" repeats Zorro.

"A spy, Madam, trained by FAPLA. It is written all over you. Practised in armed combat, are you, my little dove of peace?"

"I trained in first-aid, that's all."

"Brainwashed, child. Like the whole people, who are too stupid to understand. Even the educated, like you, Nakale, fall for it. How do they say in English?—hook, line and sinker.

"Equality . . . Justice . . . They are mere words—meaningless."

Malenga speaks to the ground, for Zorro holds her face centimetres from it. "But not *your* words." She repeats the phrase as Zorro levers down her neck. "Your words, your words!"

"My words?"

The White Wolves have never seen the Big Man caught in his stride before. "What do you mean, 'my words'? Are you suggesting my words are not to be trusted?"

"'Freedom'—isn't that your big word?"

Cardinal to himself: "Je-sus!"

"What are you implying, you insolent little witch?" This is the Chief Cockerel his men more easily recognize. In a rage—deaf and blind. "That I do not respect freedom? *I*?"

No orchestra could ever keep up with the acceleration of the silver-topped baton as it thrashes the air. "How dare you? My entire life has been devoted to one thing—the freedom of my beloved country."

Malenga shouts so loudly the dirt beneath her lips makes a pocket of air. "Then what about *my* freedom? How dare you rob me of it?"

Eyes, nose, mouth are screwed into earth.

In the deep recess of his head, Zorro describes the Big Man's mood in terms of a favourite film—*Towering Inferno*. "Kill her now, Chief—now!"

Tomas has seen enough. They are going to execute his sister. He takes aim. The branch that supports him won't stay still. The sights of his hunting gun waver in and out of line.

Can't wait.

Tomas presses the trigger.

Chapter Six

In the prison compound, Hamish hears the single gunshot, and instantly afterwards the shattering of glass. He snaps out of his gloom. He leaps to his feet—and also jumps to a conclusion: attack!

His hands are cupped; the joy in him is a tidal wave. His shout bursts on the night:

"F-A-P-L-A!"

Fellow prisoners believe him. They seize on hope, dancing with anticipation:

"F-A-P-L-A!"

The single shot is a memory, for instants later the darkness thunders with gunfire, all of it—as events will prove—coming from UNITA's own weapons.

According to the latest reports, the army of the People's Republic is hundreds of kilometres away, but inside the minds of UNITA, FAPLA is never more than a thought away.

On the parade ground they are ducking each other's fire. The majority, like their chief, lie flat on their faces, while a few bravados stay on their knees, see FAPLA in every shadow, and tracer the mopanes with wasted bullets.

The camp sentries have seen nothing, heard nothing. The road is clear. Yet they too begin to fire at the enemy within their skulls.

On his perch up in the sky, hearing not far off him the

whistle of bullets, Tomas of the Nine Lives isn't sure whether to be sorry or glad. His aim was for the Big Man. His achievement is a broken windscreen—and all this.

Now even the sentries are crying "FAPLA!"

"FAPLA my foot!" Zorro attempts to stand, but the shooting around him is too desperate. Already soldiers have been hit by their own comrades' fire.

"We're going to massacre ourselves," decides Cardinal.

"We gotta shoot our way out, Boss!" urges Musso.

"What with, you brain-damaged pig?"

"Boss?" replies the brain-damaged pig. "Where's the girl?"

Malenga is running, out of this madness. OK die—what's it matter? She swerves, skids, steps over flattened bodies, dodges—watch it, here comes Maradona.

Nobody seems to see her. She's visible, but it is invisible enemies that concern the Big Man's army. To the huts. Each second she expects the burning entry of bullets. At least it'll be over.

Side-stepping, weaving, skirting the windscreen-shattered truck, past the abandoned film projector, take-up spool still spinning; and she can hear Zorro bellowing for order.

Somewhere farther off, the cry of "FAPLA!" is stifled, and a prisoner receives a beating.

"False alarm!" Zorro has rescued the loudhailer from Maynard, the American, who has taken refuge beneath the front axles of the projector truck.

"Cease all firing . . . At once, Christ damn you all!" Finally he uses a word the Tuga-speaking soldiers can understand.

"SILÊNCIO!"

Malenga is among the thatched-roof huts, grateful for the protection of eyeless walls, but under no illusions: I've been seen. There will be no escape.

She stops, legs quivering, back against rough clay. There is moonlight. It is cold. She can see her own breath.

Despite his success in bringing the camp to order again, Zorro receives the blame. There are four dead, several wounded. The Big Man peels off his white gloves, smothered in dust.

"Look at them!" He hurls the gloves into Zorro's face. "You are finished in this camp, soldier—you and the scum that serve you.

"Finished!"

Zorro thinks he is being accused of firing the single shot which caused this fiasco. "We were stripped of our weapons, Chief, so how could we—?"

"I'm not referring to that, you white trash. You brought the curse on this place, you and your filthy mercenaries."

"Curse?—me?"

"A Nakale—you brought a Nakale, a witch, responsible for contaminating this kingdom."

Zorro considers the Big Man is getting things out of proportion. "She's just a kid, Chief. English public school —wet behind the ears."

"And where is the witch now, soldier?"

Zorro lies: "Being escorted to the compound at this very instant, Chief."

The silver-topped cane jabs into Zorro's chest. "Let that be so, Mister. Your life depends upon it."

Musso has crossed the gap between the huts, ahead of Malenga. He looks. Her eyes are tight shut. He sees nothing, pauses, turns his back, lights a cigarette, sighs, then groans, passes on.

The space he leaves tempts Malenga. She decides on the other route.

In for a penny.

She sprints towards the far end of the huts. The way is blocked. Sparkler's knife speaks: move once and die.

Hamish, beside the gate of the compound: "Don't crowd her!"

At the sight of Malenga in the distance, frog-marched by the White Wolves, his cheer had switched to a cry of protest.

"Leave her alone, you bastards!"

She is bleeding from the nose. Musso has her head wrenched back as if he wished to pluck it from her neck. The gate open, she is hurled into black dust.

"Back, please—give her air." Hamish's fellow prisoners want to help. He holds them off, lifts her by the shoulders, at the same time roaring at Zorro.

There is blood on her hands, a long cut as from a knife-blade. She has her own rage, won't be held, won't be shielded. She clutches the fence. Blood drips down her forearm. Her fingers grasp the wire and the wire is Zorro's throat:

"You'd have let him . . . You'd have stood by!"

"So what?—you escaped your fate-worse-than-death, didn't you?—thanks to Uncle Cardinal."

Hamish has ripped off the sleeve of his shirt. "Malenga, hold your hand steady."

Zorro is turning away. His mind is on beer and a dream of music.

Malenga: "I haven't finished with you, Mister!"

Mister? Twice in a night Zorro's rank has been ignored.

Malenga pulls her hand from Hamish's grasp, continues to address the retreating officer. "I want what belongs to me . . . My medical case. Now!"

Zorro gazes at the sky. Twice in a night he has been

shouted at. "You amaze me, Sheba. One minute you're kneeing Sparkler in the nuts for his perfectly natural desires, the next—"

"I want that case!"

Zorro is unmoved. "And I want my beer . . . No case!"

Cardinal tries to interpose. "We need her fit and well, Captain."

Zorro nods towards Hamish. "She's already got her medicine-man."

Now Malenga responds to Hamish's coaxing. "I blew it."

His arm is around her. "Forget it." He bandages her, then leads her to the softest spot of ground.

She sits, propped against his knee. "Thanks, medicine-man."

"I thought I'd never see you again."

They are surrounded by curious faces. Hamish introduces his new friends—most of them wounded, all of them sick: Malenga's countrymen. The shock of the evening's events takes its toll. She shivers. Is this fever coming on?

"Meet Rodrigo, Malenga. He's from up west some place."

Rodrigo smiles, nurses a useless arm. "Cangamba."

Malenga returns the smile, nods. "Moxico Province." There are tears in his eyes. "Beautiful up there." Of course. Home is always beautiful when you cannot return to it in freedom.

It dawns on her that Hamish is speaking Tuga with the prisoners. He has already learnt their stories: Josef from Luengue, family killed before his eyes; Crispus from Kunene, shoulder and arm broken by rifle butts; Michael from Cuito Cuanavale: "They took me when FAPLA turned back the big invasion. The bandits had to have their revenge —the men they took for slaves, the rest they shot down, even babes in arms . . . I would like to ask the American people, Do you know how your guns are being used in my country?"

Rodrigo takes up the argument. "The Yanks think they are fighting communists. Yet what they are doing is supporting apartheid." A glance towards Hamish. "This boy's evil system."

"I deserted, didn't I?"

Malenga is almost gone, sliding along dark corridors of sleep. She hears herself say, "You personally, we forgive."

"Thanks."

Risto from Caprivi had tried to escape. They cut off his toes. He has been reluctant to accept Hamish. He asks the youth, "Why did you wait so long?"

Hamish attempts a grin, shakes his head. "I just worked twelve hours in a store. And when I got home, I dug my Dad's patch."

"And you watched hundreds of Hitchcock films." Malenga has not intended to be harsh, but her comment hurts.

"Sure, I turned my back on things. I've no excuses." Hamish finds himself angry at her. She seems to expect so much from people. "If I'd been Black I'd have known what to do. I'd have had a cause." He looks around him. "At least I'd have had a friend in this world."

He is about to scramble away, but Malenga holds him. She says nothing. She does not look at him. She straightens his legs to form a double pillow and lays her head in his lap.

"Now try to keep very still. I'm a light sleeper." Her hand reaches for his. She lays his fingers on her forehead. "Just there, where it aches. That's nice."

"She's your friend," laughs Rodrigo.

*

How did the poem go?

I stand back from the river of blood
And discover sweet words.

Ah yes. How easy it seemed then.

They restore me like a fountain
Sprung from the desert.

I knew nothing. Now the river is my own blood. It is afire and all the words have been consumed. Words will never encompass all this evil, all this suffering. Better to watch a million films, listen to your Sony Walkman, play with your white gloves and silver-topped cane.

Julius: you're beginning to understand, Child.

No. I'm adrift in a dinghy, passing through understanding to ignorance again. Confusion.

How did it continue?

Words.
They become the stepping stones
Across the insane river . . .

No, *I* have become the insane river, unable any more to recognize one word from another. I used to like that—

. . . one by one the stones
Turn their faces towards me:
My loved ones in so many words.

Good grief, what did it *mean*? These faces? Rodrigo's shattered arm, Crispus' broken shoulder, Risto's toes?

Is that what words mean—
Like toes without feet?

Fransina: you feel things in the way that we do; that can be a curse as well as a blessing.

Sleep!

Can't sleep. Then what's this ship doing in Luanda Harbour, with great sails, a scarlet flag? And those fishermen . . . Come on, Malenga, throw the blossoms or Kianda, Goddess of the Sea, will be angry.

Instead of blossoms, Kianda,
I sprinkle on your emerald gown
All the words in my life
Which have lost their meaning.

Is 'love' the same as 'loss'? Is 'death' the same as 'joy'?

Outside in the mopane forest, the crickets have rediscovered their musicianship. A wind has risen, bristling in from the west, touching and rippling the double-winged leaves of the butterfly trees, singing through them.

"Children, what's the name of the currency of our country?"

Dédo, always first: "Kwanza!" Goodbye Dédo.

"Why that word?"

Tomas, always challenging for prime place in teacher's attention: "The name of our great river." Where are you, Tomas of the Nine Lives?

"And the tributary to that great river?"

"Lwei."

Good times. Then 'joy' meant 'love'. "How many Lwei to a Kwanza?"

"Hundred."

It's freezing yet I'm on fire. Yes, Mrs Trench, my spirit was as dark as my skin; always. In the bush I found happiness.

"*Cacimbo* means?"

"Drizzly season, Miss."

"And summer?"

"*Veraõ!*"

Such beautiful words, all gone. Only one thing matters now—to return to that; to start afresh. "Who's ever heard of *Beleizaõ*?"

Every hand jabs at the sky:

"Ice-cream, Miss!"

That is freedom, Mister Big Man; to lick your ice-cream and not have to worry in which bit of earth lies the terrorist's bomb.

Beneath the tangled mass of the butterfly tree roof, Tomas finds no escape from a dream of his own, the one which comes back again and again. Three years old, he is pulling at his mother's arm. She will not get up, won't brush the flies from her face.

The soldiers have been. Tuga is not their language, but killing is. Tomas shakes her face. The eyes will not open. Somebody comes from behind, lifts him up, has to disengage his grasp, finger by finger.

He struggles, for they are throwing her into a pit. There are many others. He is left alone among the fires. Even now, the smell of petrol haunts his nostrils.

"Mamma!"

Hamish will deny that he has slept. He has been in conversation, lively and painful, with Dirk, his fellow runaway, and he is telling him about Malenga.

She's the sort who'll marry a diplomat or a surgeon. Even you, Dirk, you'd be in with a chance. Anyhow, she's left with me, the Great Explorer, Okavango Oscar, alias Troopy Four-eyes, plain as a cabbage. If the wind's blowing that way, they'd smell me in Durban: grocer's runner.

I've not a chance . . . and yet.

Can you fall in love with a girl on the strength of her bandaging your hand? Perhaps not—but what about handcuffs? Just like in *The Thirty-Nine Steps*, handcuffs have forged a bond, as they did with Robert Donat and Madeleine Carroll.

"That's why I like you, Hamish Ross," says Dirk. "You're the sort the world's left behind."

"Oh?"

"Like it's left the Kalahari Bushmen behind."

"There's where you're wrong, Mr Philosopher. The San people have much to teach us. One day the world will catch up with *them*."

"It's a long way to Kalahari."

"Not as the fish-eagle flies . . . Malenga, would you be interested—I mean in coming with me?"

"I thought explorers were lonely souls who preferred their own company."

"Aren't poets?"

Sunrise, and Henry Maynard, secret agent, is dreaming of home: a ticker-tape welcome for his services to peace and freedom across the globe.

Time to hang up your walking boots, Mister Mischief.

The dream has survived ambush by mosquitos. He has so far shut out the drone of troop reinforcements arriving through the small hours.

Yet the dream of glory is sundered for ever—at the very moment the President is awarding Maynard the Congressional Medal—by an uninvited guest any civilized country would already have deported.

"Hargreaves . . . What the devil?"

"Look at this, Maynard!" Zorro yanks the Congressional Medal winner back to reality.

"Don't you ever knock, soldier?"

"That's the point—I'm a soldier no longer."

Maynard's hand, the one which only moments ago lay in the honoured presidential palm, is wrenched forward. His elbow burns. A ball of white paper alights like a wounded dove on his fingers.

"Read it, Maynard—or do you already know what it says?"

"*Calma*, as the Tugas say." Maynard rights himself, gets up, crosses to a table where there is a bottle and a glass. He takes a second glass from a drawer.

Zorro speaks as if Maynard were at the other end of Angola. "The best soldier in this creep's army is assigned to escort duty. Me, escort duty!"

"Drink, Captain?"

"Carrying a load of half-dead jerks into the arsehole of the world."

"Namibia is not to be spoken of in such terms, Captain. Namibia is to be the new Land of the Free."

"Yeah? And for how long before we turn her into another Angola, another Mozambique?" Zorro downs his drink. "I want *this* war, Maynard. *My* war."

"You owe it to your kid brother, right?"

"Exactly."

"And to do that you want to kill every Angolan, correct?"

"Every last one."

Maynard sits down. The worst is over. He fears Zorro. He admires him. He dislikes him. "And how many Angolans did your kid brother put out of their misery before FAPLA caught him and shot him?"

The American stares out of the window at the lightening sky. "What is it about you Brits?"

"I'm not British. I'm Boer, through and through."

Maynard lets the matter go. "Your kid brother followed in your footsteps, Mike, didn't he? He couldn't wait to use the flame-thrower, lob bombs into schoolhouses. You're angry because *he* paid the price, not you."

"They never gave him a chance."

"Rubbish. They caught him. They tried him. He confessed." Maynard feels robbed. Drink and dreams—they're the only luxury left; the only meaning. He refills Zorro's glass. "Listen, those half-dead jerks are sandbags round a prize worth a princess's ransom—Julius Nakale's daughter.

"Think of yourself for a change, Captain. You put your hand in the pond and came out with the Koh-i-noor diamond. And there'll be a percentage in it for you. Think of that when you're heading south."

Another drink: the heat has arrived. "Is she that valuable?"

"She's ace, she's bait." Maynard dabs his forehead. "A little bird tells me that Mandela will soon be back on the streets of Soweto. But it's Nakale we want. He's young, ruthless and bright—and he's the king-in-waiting. He's the one we fear the most."

"So this kid is your hot-line to Nakale."

"You got it." Maynard sighs at the thought of another day of this heat, rolling over him in unremitting waves. There is something else. "Things are on the move, Mike. Changing —the whole scenario."

"What's that supposed to mean?"

"It's time to call off the dogs. You mercenaries are history now—see how even Big Man hates you. Leave Angolans to fight Angolans, Blacks against Blacks. In any event, our business is switching to Namibia, to keep the commies out of there."

"What's wrong with Cardinal doing the escort job? Why me?"

"Because you're bad news, chum. Killers are out, diplomats are in. We're in to Hearts and Minds now—got me?"

The spirit has gone out of Zorro. He too is wounded by the heat. "I'll need assurances."

"You got 'em."

"What about the fourteen Blacks on the list?"

"Fourteen *dying* Blacks."

"Meaning?"

"They're contaminated. They've been working on those toxic dumps."

"Where's that coming from?"

"All over. It's big business, chum. Helps pay for the Big Man's cigars. After all, Angola's full of open spaces and the world's desperate to get rid of its industrial shit."

"How far do I cart these guys?"

"Out of sight."

"Maynard, you're a bigger villain than I am."

Ignoring Zorro's remark, the American goes on briskly. "We're expecting a British film crew today. For them, this camp's got to put on a good face. Civilized. That means we want no unsightly details—an empty prison compound for a start."

The American accompanies Zorro to the door, shakes a reluctant hand. "Am I right, about today's world, Mike—get the image in focus, and the truth takes care of itself?"

"Bastard!"

Sunrise, and Tomas has buried his hunting gun at the edge of the butterfly woods. He has been observing the parked Land Rover for some time, and listening to the English voices of two women and a man, poring over a map spread across the vehicle's bonnet.

The contents of Tomas's English-Portuguese dictionary are about to become useful. He stands, a long shadow away; still, as if he were stalking antelope.

"You are English, yes?"

"Thank God—there's somebody!"

The hot breeze coming up from the desert rattles at the map.

They are looking for the camp of the Big Man. Peace is in the air. Tomas of the Nine Lives wishes to enter the camp of the enemy to find his sister Malenga.

He smiles. "You very lost maybe?"

"We very lost absolutely." Celia Bennett, director of the film crew, is tall, handsome, greying. Skin flushed with uncustomary heat, hair bundled untidily behind her head, she is dressed in combat jacket and a pair of smart russet trousers more appropriate for the Luanda promenade than the bush.

She introduces Geoff, her cameraman, and Paula, her sound-recordist. "We're looking for the camp of UNITA."

Tomas nods, rubs his stomach.

"He's hungry," divines Geoff.

"I speak Tuga and Umbundu. Also, one little smidgeon Mbundu."

Paula laughs, "Smidgeon? Has he swallowed a dictionary."

Tomas beams. Thank you, Sister. Smidgeon word make friends.

"Our guide ran off," Celia explains. "Afraid of UNITA."

"All people afraid of UNITA."

"But not you?"

Paula has removed her dark glasses, wipes sweat from her face. "Give him something to eat, Celia, before we lose him too."

Chapter Seven

"Not this time, Squeamish!" Zorro separates Hamish from Malenga by the whole length of the truck. "You two are divorced, as from now."

There are sixteen prisoners on board; fourteen of them on their last journey to anywhere.

In the daylight Malenga has noticed how ill her comrades are. There has been nothing to eat and only a mouthful of sun-scalded water for each prisoner. There'd be salt tablets in the medical case, but this has been left behind.

"Cheer up!" grinned Hamish as they had climbed the truck, steadying themselves against roof spars roped with canvas. "Things could be worse."

"Oh?" This boy is crazy.

Zorro has called him a dead man. The words have cast a cold shadow over Malenga's heart. But Hamish joked: "That means I can come back into this world as a flamingo. Much better idea. Then I'll wing it over the Delta."

The forests of mopane have given way to scrubland, flat, featureless—sweltering. The breeze is desert-sprung, and this landscape is the prologue to desert, sprinkled with lonely copses of acacia.

Colours shimmer and shake in the eye, light-beaten, lid-burning. Lips are chapped, coming out in sores. At least talk.

"What are they, Hamish?" Malenga points at the great yellow flowers weighing down the tree branches.

"Camelthorn."

"The rains are coming," says Rodrigo.

"To your left, Malenga—shepherd tree." How can he be so chirpy? "You know what they call the great baobab?"

"Monkey bread tree."

Musso isn't in a mood for quizzes on trees. "Shut up the both of you!"

Hamish steals a point. "And that's blackthorn."

"I said shut up, boy." Musso aims his Kalashnikov at Hamish's chest.

"Just talking to the flowers, Sir."

Malenga fears for him. Somehow Hamish's desperate situation does the opposite of taming him. He wants to provoke them, try them out.

Is this what he meant by 'thinking of something'?

Hamish has turned his attention to the silent Sparkler, even nudged the soldier's calf with his foot. "Bad tactics, Sparkler—your captain separating us two enemies of the state."

Sparkler does not speak, but he fixes Hamish with a gaze which only the glare of the sun, and the sudden watering of his eyes, brings to an end.

"You know why?—because absence makes the heart grow fonder . . . Right, Malenga?"

Musso, roasting pork in the heat, bellows: "Shut up! One more word out of you, Smart Guy, and you'll catch a bullet in your other hand."

Malenga bars the reply that might have forced Musso to carry out his threat. "Please, Hamish."

"For your sake, but not for his."

From the cab of the truck, driven by Cardinal, comes Zorro's music, played on a cassette tape recorder stolen from Roberto. The air is loaded with martial trumpets, with the ocean-roar of drums.

Hamish forgets his promise, shouts at Zorro: "Theme music from *Apocalypse Now*, 1979, Coppola directing, and starring Brando, Sheen and Duvall." He turns to Malenga but at the same time attempting to elicit Musso's interest. "Wagner, that is. When the choppers are going in to beat the hell out of some innocent kimbo."

"Very appropriate," comes in Malenga, swiftly, hoping her interjection might check the steam issuing from Musso's temper.

"And that guy," goes on Hamish, jerking thumb and fist in the direction of Zorro, "is just an overgrown kid."

To Malenga's surprise and relief, Musso seems to agree. He shrugs. Hamish presses home his advantage. "Thinks he's hero of a movie, doesn't he?"

Musso allows himself the trace of a smile. "B-movie!"

Hot, unbelievably; indescribably. Midday and the dregs of Malenga's energy evaporate. No more conversations. One word would be so heavy it'd tip me over on to my face. My breath's burning my cheeks. The air's being hoovered out of me.

With all that water, the Okavango Delta must be cool. Blue water, white water, things floating, mirrored. I'd pick up the sky in my hands, drink the heavens.

Nectar!

I'd splash it over my eyes. Absence makes the heart grow fonder: true, Julius; true, Fransina, though we quarrel most of the time when we meet.

Opening my eyes again, I'd be able to see for ever. All

things would be clear. And when the sunset turned the Okavango to a scarlet miracle, I'd make love to this boy.

I'd like that.

She has noticed tears in the eyes of the prisoner Michael. This is his country—a shattered land. He is seeing the territory of his birth for the last time, its desolation: bomb-mutilated villages, uninhabited save for wildcats—peering in terror from deep shadows; the burnt-out shells of farm-steads, fields turned to baked dust; overturned trucks in ditches; a fire-blackened bus; the carcass of a tractor—that rarest of all vehicles in this, the poorest region of Angola—slumped on shell-bent axles.

Where have they fled to
These farmers whose home
Was named—even by them—
The Land at the End of the Earth,
Leaving their hoes
Like stick insects
Against the callous
Beauty of the sky?

Written all over this landscape is the message: the Boers were here. To ease this pain, translate it into images; compose, write it, shift it into the sanctuary of words:

The Black Death was here.
It came armed with steel
Bearing flags of hate:
Its deadly scythe eclipsed the sun.
Its very wind
Swept the people into space.

Who are you missing, Michael, that in this heat you can find water enough for tears? Across once-irrigated fields lie the corpses of cattle, too many to have died merely from neglect. Yet the heat is so intense that the vultures have yielded the rich pickings, for shelter under distant trees.

Malenga breaks the truce of silence, aiming her words at Musso. "Are you proud of all this?"

Mussolini raises his head from a paralysis of heat. "When the Blacks get above themselves, this is what happens to 'em, Nakale. Otherwise, they'd never know who was boss." He nods at his own wisdom. "That's what life's about, deciding who's boss. Ask the Captain!"

Malenga aims to have the last word. "You don't *really* believe that nonsense, do you?"

"Nonsense?" Musso stares at her through sweat. He looks about him. "I don't believe anything any more, sweetie. Nor will you when you get to my age." He grins at his own wit. "*If* you get to my age."

Musso's comment seems to confirm the fears Rodrigo had expressed at the beginning of the journey: "They will not take us far, these men." He had put his hands together, fingertips touching—and prayed.

I'm valuable, they won't kill me.

Oh no?

Can't think any more; all at once everything is aching —head, stomach, legs, arms; shaking, head the weight of a hippo. Could this be Angolan Anguish?

Garcia: "Bacillary dysentery. You feel worse than death. It could last a fortnight."

Spare me that.

All you can do is try to be cheerful.

Hi, Fransina, here's Cheerful. Sorry you'll not be getting this month's letter. I'm in a bit of a spot, almost as serious as Angolan Anguish. Remember giving me that postcard of the old candy floss seller in Lubango? My pal Rodrigo once bought his kid some. He's like you, Fransina, doesn't know where his daughter has got to.

There's another thing. I've met up with this boy called Hamish. We got acquainted via a pair of handcuffs. When he's not wearing his glasses, he's quite handsome. Reddish hair and—oh—he's white, though his freckles cast a question-mark over his racial purity.

Joke.

South African too: do you mind? Don't worry, we'll probably not be seeing each other again after today. Worth mentioning, though. He's offered to take me cruising down the Okavango.

Tell Dad to expect a ransom note. But don't pay it because they'll kill me anyway. I talk too loud.

The Big Man got his gloves dirty.

One last thing I'd like you to know—all this has not been a waste, though it's been a nightmare.

I no longer stand
In the margins
Of other people's lives,
In other people's cities.

This land is my space.
It surrounds me, embraces me
With the warmth
Of its suffering
And its joy.

Passing on through eternal scrubland—that's not the right word: screaming through it. Everything's melting, one colour bleeding into another. The coating's wearing off my eyes.

Suddenly, wide awake, grasping at air. Without warning the truck has braked, pulled off into acacia scrub; halts.

Zorro leaps from the cab. "Fetch the prisoners down, Fat Man."

"What's up, Boss?"

"Campfire smoke ahead," explains Cardinal. "Possibly FAPLA."

Hamish jumps the queue to be beside Malenga. For helping her down, he earns a hug. "Now they're for it."

"I can't see no smoke, Boss."

"We're not taking any risks." FAPLA: and Zorro is respectful; even afraid. "OK, Musso, you looking for some action?"

"Like what, Boss?"

"Like scouting, sniffing 'em out."

"Not me, Boss—please! Remember my asthma."

Zorro has no real intention of detailing Musso as scout. He nods at Cardinal. "Check them over, Sergeant."

The prisoners are allowed to seek shelter in the frail shade of the acacias. Hamish digs through a crust of baked earth with his fingers. "Here, this'll ease the heat." He offers Malenga damp soil. "All over your face and neck."

She smiles. "I've got that special sort of skin, remember."

He feels a fool. "Bright ideas!"

"Don't worry. I appreciate your concern. Aren't you going to take your own advice?"

Hamish removes his glasses. The soil isn't wet enough but

he goes on plastering himself. "If I had your special sort of skin, Malenga, would you like me better?"

She is silent, though her eyes do not leave his face.

"Said something wrong, have I?"

"I could ask you the same question."

"The trouble is, however hard I try, I can never really know what it's like to be you."

She takes dry earth, powders it in her hand. Then she opens Hamish's good hand and pours earth into it. "Gold dust . . . You just go on being yourself."

Funny, that was what Dirk once said to him. Appreciating this vote of confidence, Hamish gives rein to his natural impatience. "OK, so when are we going to make our run for it?"

Malenga stares into the bush, into the land that the gods forgot, into skin-stripping heat, towards measureless, waterless vistas. She hasn't enough energy to shake her head.

Hamish replaces his glasses, leans on his elbow. "Nothing's worse than not trying."

Sparkler calls from his guard position south of the clearing. "Sarge come back!" A moment later, he adds, "He show bad face, Boss."

Musso decides, "It's FAPLA all right." He turns on Malenga. "This bitch has brought us bad luck ever since we took her."

Cardinal emerges between the trees. He flashes both sets of fingers twice.

"Je-sus—we're outnumbered, Boss!"

There is a stirring among the prisoners: fear and hope in equal proportions; in Malenga, only terror. Her inner eye is blinded by a vision of carnage.

We're a handicap. They'll get rid of us.

She is standing, Hamish beside her, good hand tight round hers. They watch Zorro and Cardinal retreat into shade. They pace in a circle, Zorro gesturing, pointing—first at the troop of government soldiers down the road, their camp fire pencilling grey into blue, then at the prisoners.

Hamish: "They're going to kill us."

"One shot will bring FAPLA running."

"You're forgetting Sparkler's knife, and they all carry machetes."

Zorro is saying, "We can turn this show to our advantage. We've never got this close to FAPLA without 'em knowing."

"Four guns against twenty, Boss."

"Tell me, why do we kidnap these vermin? So FAPLA will come after us, do battle, lose half their squad—right?"

"While we lose three-quarters." Cardinal's view is that they should board the truck. "Do a detour. After all, we've orders."

"Still thinking about the old pension, Cardinal—playing safe?"

"By the book, Sir."

Musso suggests his own plan. "Boss? How's about we wait for dark when we can lighten our load a bit. Then hightail it back to camp, join the action?" Musso knows his captain.

Zorro has already decided. "I want shut of this company. They give me the creeps." He evades Cardinal's gaze. "This is a dirty little war, Sergeant, so what do a few extra corpses matter?" He has not bothered to lower his voice. His intentions are public knowledge.

Zorro summons Sparkler, orders him to shift the prisoners into the centre of the glade. "On their knees, hands behind their backs."

Cardinal protests, points at Malenga and Hamish. "They're witnesses to this, Boss."

"Who'll take any notice of them, Cardinal? She's a Marxist spy, daughter of a terrorist. He's a leper for the rest of his days . . . Unless, of course, *you* report us." Zorro's AK-47 is directed at Cardinal's belly. "But then think of the poor Missus back in Brandfort."

Malenga can hardly breathe for the pounding of blood in her chest. Her head is rocking. The nausea of Angolan Anguish is overtaken by the nausea of horror. She tries to speak, but no voice comes.

I must act.

"Hamish!" That much she gets out. He is close to her. To Cardinal, an appeal: "Sergeant!" To Zorro, "You could let them go . . . They're nothing to you!"

"They're enemy."

"There's no *point*!"

Hamish: "Nobody'll say anything."

Zorro prides himself in never shirking a debate. "Listen, Sheba, I'm doing these prisoners a favour. They're dying. They have inhaled the poison—look at them. It's a mercy . . ."

A mercy: like Dédo?

"And these bonzos won't die in vain, I assure you. The shooting will bring FAPLA who'll join all their comrades in the big socialist paradise in the sky."

Malenga clutches Hamish's hand, presses it tightly till her nails scar his palm. She tugs him in the direction of the other prisoners, the condemned.

"Us too, then!"

Hamish fights on, even though he has moved into the sights of Musso's and Sparkler's guns. "These men have kids—families. Let them die happy!"

The tears blind Malenga. She kneels beside Rodrigo. Josef from Luengue makes room for Hamish.

Am I crazy—that I could almost laugh now? She takes Hamish's arm. So what's all this fuss about the colour of our skins?

Zorro is unimpressed. "Very well. The choice is yours. In your own time, gentlemen, take aim."

Musso and Sparkler obey.

Cardinal has also raised his gun, but it is trained upon Captain Mike Hargreaves, the Mighty Zorro. "Sir, our orders are to bring those two back alive."

Zorro does not doubt Cardinal's intentions. He behaves as though he expected this to happen. "Say goodbye to your stripes, Sergeant." To Musso, "You're witness, Mussolini, to the insubordination of this soldier."

"Boss?"

"Fetch them out of there, Fat Man . . . Quick, before Sparkler and me forget we're gentlemen."

Musso approaches, Kalashnikov poised at the hip. "On your feet, you bleeding little martyrs!"

Without any warning, Hamish launches himself at the Fat Man, gun ignored. Musso fires. The bullet bites sand. They are rolling over each other, straining for leverage to release blows.

Sparkler shoots into the pack. Risto of Caprivi falls. The gun's free, but Hamish has no strength to match the bulk and force of his opponent.

Malenga is down, from knees to stomach, reaching, pulling. The AK-47 is along her body. Zorro fires. Rodrigo from Cangamba drops.

Zorro aims again.

Malenga's left hand grips the barrel, lifts it from earth. Her fingers search, find, squash the trigger.

Captain Hargreaves falls back from his own aim. The bullet enters his head. He sways, for a second. His own knees strike dust. For another second he remains upright, then topples backwards against his own boots.

Malenga is up, screaming at the prisoners:

"Run for it!"

There is a blow from behind, across her head.

At the fall of their leader, the White Wolves are stone. They await orders, but from their commander there will be no more orders.

Ignored, twelve prisoners spread into the forest, their arms and elbows pumping shadows, their hands snatching at liberty.

The only voice is Cardinal's:

"My God!"

His rifle is pressed into Malenga's flesh below the ear. "Remove your finger from the trigger, Miss Nakale!"

Chapter Eight

It slides over her head, the sky; chicken-roasting, oven-steaming; stuffed with peppers bursting; hammer sky. Looking up, a mistake. One mistake after another, Malenga Nakale. When will you ever learn?

Stubborn.

No bird backs into a hole: old Angolan proverb. But you did, all the way, and then some.

After the gloom of the cell, the light of the parade ground beats her blind.

"Wait here."

Yellow sand, a sick colour; unhealthy sand. There is a breeze. Kalahari, are you out there somewhere? Rattling at the flag above the compound. Big place, divided off.

Beyond the next roll of barbed wire, a silent crowd of watchers. Forced labour? Women, all: hi comrades! It's me they're waving at. Stick up your hands; good. Shake them.

The women are cheering: bless you, sisters!

"Forward!"

Sand exchanged for wooden planks, like the Medical Centre steps, cruel to the knees. Right turn, halt at the door.

"Wait!"

Eyes can't keep up with the changes of light; can scarcely make out the printed words: MILITARY COURT. Door hinges need oiling. They whine in protest at the heat.

"Prisoner Nakale, Sir." A push. "Step forward. Address the bench."

Address the . . . Once I'd have smiled. Address the bench: hello, Mister Bench.

Once.

Up a step. There is a rail, use it.

Three soldiers are seated behind a trestle table; officers. A South African flag hangs on the wall behind them.

In the centre of the ceiling, just below the rafters, a slow fan trundles; useless, not even budging the flies.

No jury.

"You may commence the case for the prosecution, Lieutenant Noupoort."

A young man: sporting a well-combed moustache, to make him look more mature. "Thank you, Colonel." To Malenga, "Address your words not to me but to Colonel Christianson, you understand?"

The Colonel's head is high-domed, an upturned bell, a beacon, sweat-polished.

What's it with moustaches?

"Does the prisoner speak English?"

"She received an English public school education, Colonel."

"I see. Not an unusual practice among Marxist revolutionaries to buy the best education for their offspring." Smiles; too hot for anything more demonstrative.

Noupoort bustles, bristles. "Sir, it is the custom of the court for the accused to state his or her own name, but the prisoner refuses to answer to any other than, well—"

"Than what?"

"The Queen of Sheba, Sir."

"I don't care a damn whether she's the Queen of

Hearts—this court demands her name, and from her own lips."

Noupoort is not happy. "She is stubborn, Sir. From the moment she was brought in, an unco-operative prisoner. Rest assured, she is Malenga Nakale."

"Please . . ." Malenga sways, grasps the rail in front of her. Rail shaking, prisoner shaking. "Can't stand."

"What is the matter with her?"

"She claims sickness, Sir—Angolan Anguish, I believe they call it."

Christianson detests Angolan anything. "Stand she must!" He raps the table with his officer's baton. Malenga notices —it has no silver tip. "As for refusing to give her name, I do not blame her, for it resounds across the civilized world in infamy! . . . Continue with the case, Lieutenant."

Malenga hears confirmation: you are a spy of the Marxist government of Angola. You plotted the death of a South African officer. You shot Koevoet Captain Michael Hargreaves in the back at point-blank range.

"Where exactly did the shooting take place?"

"On buffer-zone territory, Sir, while Captain Hargreaves and his men were on peaceful border patrol."

"I was taken!" Malenga fights to give life to her voice; to uncrack it. "I was kidnapped, taken—"

"Be silent, Nakale. You will be permitted to make your defence later."

Malenga's legs give way. She falls with an untidy bang.

"Silence in court! . . . Look, Noupoort, what is the matter with her?"

"She fought with her warders, Sir. She is a wildcat . . . Sir, all this information will be made clear in due course."

Guards scoop her to her feet, prop her against the rail. "A

trick, Sir . . . To appeal to your sympathy. She's full of them. Talks to her guards, tries to wheedle them from their duties. All the time, calculating, attempting bare-faced subversion of those in authority over her."

Christianson dabs away sweat. "Economise on the speech-making, Noupoort. She's up for murder, not revolution."

Malenga recognizes a small miracle—her strength is returning; adrenalin, the fire in the blood. "I was kidnapped on Angolan soil. The doctor I worked with was killed by Koevoet."

"Fabrication, Colonel."

"Of course. Now be silent, Nakale. And stand up straight."

They are discussing the murder weapon. I'm sorry for you, Zorro. But more sorry for myself. Taking your life—worthless, I almost said—I've destroyed my own. There will be no peace in my head from now on.

"Who trained you to use the Russian Kalashnikov so expertly?"

"It was the Fat Man's gun."

"Fat Man?"

Noupoort: "One of Hargreaves' men, Sir. And the woman is lying. The South African Defence Force do not carry communist weapons."

Persistent: "I fired Musso's gun!"

"Musso?"

"Same person, Sir. Hargreaves loved to give people nick-names. It endeared him to his men."

Malenga is asking, "Then how did I?—"

"Get hold of a weapon, Sheba—sorry, Nakale? By smuggling it on board the transport vehicle."

Christianson recognizes the snare counsel for the prosecution has set for himself. "All that we need to know,

Noupoort, is that there was a gun, that the prisoner fired it, that it killed a man of heroic stature and that this wrongdoer will not see the light of freedom till she walks out on a stick."

Blood slow again, fire faded. Eyes stinging, ears aching. Head gone bell-ringing.

Walk out on a stick. I'd sooner die.

Pains shoot from her ankles into her calves, making them quiver, making the kneecaps shake.

Hamish, if you could see me now.

"In this crime, Sir, she was aided and abetted by Ross, Hamish, the deserter tried and sentenced yesterday. According to witnesses, they had formed a personal bond, despite the differences in their colour, race and culture.

"As you will recall, it was Ross who distracted the unfortunate Captain Hargreaves while the accused shot him."

"Lies!" Screaming now. "Zorro was on the point of executing fourteen prisoners."

"Zorro?"

"The Captain's nickname for himself, Sir. He was known for his sense of humour."

"Fourteen prisoners—he'd lined them up, he—"

"Silence, Nakale!" Christianson calls to the guard. "Gag the prisoner . . . I warned you, Nakale. The first law of this court is order. And it is the first law of my nation."

The clerk to the court counts among his properties one Gag, for the Use Of. It is applied by the first guard while the second holds Malenga's arms behind her with a grip that threatens to tear the muscles from the bone.

Funny how a gag is two opposite things. One chokes you into silence, the other makes people laugh. Then there's a gaggle: you loved that word, Tomas; went round all day saying it. Gaggle, gaggle, giggle, goggle.

Where are you now my little brother?

Malenga's enforced silence does not bring silence in court. From out there, beyond the middle wire of the camp, there has begun a chanting. It is the women labourers, and their voices are rising in harmony for Malenga.

She can just make out the words:

Cou-rage, Si-ster, put a-side your fear . . .

Colonel Christianson appeals to his all-male colleagues. "What's going on with those women?"

"They have heard about the accused, Sir. It is their way of expressing solidarity."

"With an assassin?"

"With a Nakale, Sir."

Christianson is wilting in the heat. He passes his hand over his forehead and the fingers drip sweat. "Please move things along, Lieutenant."

Cou-rage, Si-ster, put a-side your fear,
Join us in the fight for li-ber-ty . . .

"Hyenas!"

Raise with us the burn-ing spear,
March with us to vic-to-ry!

Cardinal, the witness, has taken the stand. He will not make things worse, he will not make them better. In answer to the question, "Were you at any time, in contravention of the Peace Protocol, on patrol in enemy—excuse me, Angolan—territory?" Cardinal had shaken his head.

"I am not permitted to say, Sir, in open court, as I was on a High Security mission."

"Quite so."

Noupoort: "Would I be correct in saying, Sergeant Bishop, that Captain Hargreaves was convinced Nakale was a member of FAPLA, one of its highly trained youth cadres?"

"He made a statement to that effect, Sir, yes." A momentary glance, eyes reaching out to Malenga. "Though . . . she never struck me that way."

"I see. Then you disagreed with the judgment of your superior?"

A stare, this time for Noupoort, contempt answering contempt. "She was a nurse, pure and simple. A good one, too."

Thank you, Cardinal. I forgive you.

"Yet she used a Kalashnikov, firing it like a professional when the Captain's back was turned."

"She just fired it, Sir. That's all. She believed she was saving the lives of the prisoners—"

"Prisoners? What prisoners?"

"I'm sorry—the labour unit."

"That is better, Sergeant. Your task was to transport workmen, right?"

"Sir."

"And what possible reason would Captain Hargreaves have to execute precious workmen, considering the labour shortages we are suffering at present? Would that not be an insane thing to do? Speak up, Sergeant Bishop."

"Yes Sir."

"Yes Sir what?"

"It would be an insane thing to do."

"Exactly," beams Noupoort in triumph. "Nakale, do you wish to question the witness?"

Eyes filled with tears, Malenga desires only one more look into Cardinal's heart, but the gate that leads there is closing: his eyes have switched to the ground.

She shakes her head.

Cardinal hesitates before stepping from the witness stand. Colonel Christianson chooses to interpret this as a response to the chorus of women:

Cou-rage, Si-ster, be not bought nor sold
We are count-less as des-ert sand.

"My feelings too, Sergeant. On your way out, gather a few idle hands and go quell the choir." Smiles from Christianson: quell the choir? Not bad in this heat.

"That is the case for the prosecution, Sir." With the back of his hand Noupoort removes a drop of sweat which has hung from his nose. "The accused may summon her witnesses." A grin—and an even better gag than quelling the choir.

Pins and needles in her lips. I can taste blood. Must fix an appointment with my dentist to see about my gums.

"Or did all your witnesses run off into the bush, Miss Nakale?"

Everybody having fun.

Suddenly grieving for Hamish. You nearly made it, Great Escaper. But you fell into bad company. Mine. I'm surprised they've not also accused me of witchcraft.

She is permitted to release her mouth from the gag. To their astonishment, "Yes . . . My fellow prisoner, Hamish Ross. He is my witness."

Heat unbearable, courtroom suffused with a white glaze,

an elephant's weight cobweb of it, fly swollen, sleep-deep. The choir has been quelled. The women are being led, protesting, back to the quarry workings.

Yet they strike up their chorus again and their words float down the heat ripples of the morning:

Cou-rage, Si-ster, put a-side your fear,
Join us in the fight for Li-ber-ty.
Raise with us the burn-ing spear,
March with us to vic-to-ry!

Maybe I will. Nakale for ever! Straighten up. "I demand my witness!"

Hamish Ross has also talked to too many prisoners. He is deemed likely to foment trouble, so they have put him in solitary. They call it the Steamer, a wood-framed structure no bigger than an outside lavatory, with a sloping roof of corrugated metal.

Like in the film, the one they shoved Paul Newman in for thumbing his nose at authority. Brain's going—can't remember the title. He swallowed all those eggs, didn't he?

"There's no seat."

"You stand."

"They put Paul Newman in one of these."

"Shut up and get in."

Eight years for desertion. Five for aiding and abetting the enemy in the murder of a South African officer.

I'll think of something.

The Steamer itself is condemned to solitary confinement, permitted only the dark companionship of its own shadow.

Good of the camp doctor to give me some specs. I look a mess. He probably felt sorry for me.

You got a son, Doc? Doing well, is he, back in Durban? Another ginger-nut, probably.

"You're not very resentful—that's surprising."

"My own fault, Doc. Entirely."

Yes, admit it, Sheep Brain, things'd have been easier if you'd not spent nights howling like a wolf at the moon:

"Ma-len-ga! Ma-len-ga!"

You've got to, though, if you love a person. It's called giving comfort.

During his own trial, Hamish had caused grave offence: he had told the truth. There had been broad hints of an easy ride—"Play ball with the prosecution, laddie, and we'll consider mitigating circumstances."

Mitigating circumstances? I'd not consider them even if I knew what they were.

"Use your head, son. There are ways and means."

You don't understand, do you?

"Border region my ass," he had asserted (sorry, Mother, about the bad language), "those Crowbar guys were in the middle of Angola, shooting everything that moved. The Captain himself said he liked to notch up ten corpses a day and—"

"Silence in court! Not only a deserter, Colonel, but an inveterate liar."

"You're the lie, Mister!"

Shouldn't have said that. But it was to be the later exchange which condemned Hamish Ross.

"Are you forgetting the duty you owe to your country, Ross?"

Since his desertion, and more intensely since he became

friends with Malenga, Hamish had come to consider his country a bad idea.

"I owe no duty to an evil empire." He had wondered whether he would have the nerve to do this, lift up his hand, address the bench—he too liked that, *address* it—and shout:

"Down with apartheid—everywhere!"

Steamer? This stinking hole is wrongly named. It's a smelter, Gas Mark five hundred and rising . . . Somebody shit in here. "Get off, flies! Vamoosh!"

Malenga gazes at a figure smothered in grime, peppered with bruises, swellings. "Hello, Hamish!" I go over, me, my head, my life; down the great gorges of Tundavala. Hamish, you made me happy. I only asked for you so I could see you.

"No questions, Your Honour."

"No questions? Then why the devil did you request the presence of this miscreant?"

Hamish speaks. He'll not get another chance. "Because we love each other." He grins. "That's why."

One day I'll drink to that grin. In the tricky light, grin becomes raft, drifting through wild promises. The Okavango flood is slow down the great Panhandle.

Come with me. Forget the world.

"Take the little turd away," commands Christianson. "And double his ration in the Steamer."

Over his shoulder, Hamish shouts, "Don't worry, Malenga—I'll think of something!"

The tears shake her.

The American stands back from the stench of her cell. "Je-sus, Doctor, is this the way to treat prisoners? And this young filly is a celebrity." Henry Maynard leans in, as usual mopping a sore head. "Malenga Nakale?" He speaks to her as if he has never set eyes on her before.

In a sense, he hasn't: not in this condition.

"My name's Maynard, United Nations observer."

"Stand up when you're spoken to," snaps the Doctor.

"Easy with the bedside manner, Doctor."

She is escorted across the compound, doctor ahead, Maynard close behind. "Christ, girl, what got into you? Sooner or later somebody else would have topped Hargreaves."

Suddenly, all things gleaming white—clean; a Medical Centre to remind her of that destroyed by fire. How long ago—in another life?

"Patch her up, Doc, and dress her up . . . Miss Nakale, your little deserter friend is going to be proud of you, so I want you to behave yourself . . . I've fixed up a nice team of English media people to interview you.

"Soon you'll be on telly, flashed up bright and breezy on screens from Manchester to Minneapolis, not the least in the United Nations building where we expect a certain Julius Nakale to show some interest."

"Why did they postpone my sentencing—had you something to do with that?"

"Procedure, my dear."

"I won't talk."

"For starters, Doc, a good scrub down."

Is there never any privacy? Soap, thanks. Hardly recognize it. Clothes: blue shirt.

"We don't stock bras."

Maynard, watching, marvelling. His laugh is always a half sigh. "Nakales are too proud to need support, right, Malenga?"

Loose trousers, cotton, smooth. And plimsoles, almost new.

"That's much better."

She is thinking hard, the desperate prisoner: calculating survival. "I've not been fed since yesterday morning."

The doctor protests. "That's not true, Mr Maynard. Prisoners are fed morning and evening."

"You call that feeding? The guards open the cell door and chuck the food at you. You can't even pick it out of the sludge."

Prisoners learn to use their wits, their only strength: make promises—you eat. When you've eaten—break promises. Malenga promises she will talk to the film people.

"They're impartial," claims Maynard. "You'll get British fair play."

"Spare me that."

"Sorry, I'd forgotten you got your schooling over there."

The message she must convey to the camera is simple: she must admit to her name, say nothing about the kidnap and make clear she is being treated humanely by the South African authorities.

Finally, she must appeal to her parents for help with her release.

"I will never be released."

"*We* know that, not for a decade or two—but there will be no mention of the little matter of homicide."

Maynard senses that the spirit of rebellion has been extinguished. He signals for food to be brought.

Malenga wolfs bread, cheese, fruit; pockets a wedge of fruit cake wrapped in cling-film; drains the glass of orange juice and asks for more.

"Give it to her, Doc." Maynard is feeling pleased with himself. He understands human nature.

The attention of both men is distracted by a group of prisoners being marched across the compound. "Know who they are, Doctor?"

"Rebels, I believe."

"Yes, today's rebels—tomorrow's government. In present circumstances, you're making a terrible mistake holding them like this."

"I think we know what we're doing, Mr Maynard."

"Maybe, but I've advised your commandant to double the guard, night and day, from now on."

Malenga is led through the dazzling light of the drill square to the commandant's office where the filmed interview is to take place. More luxury—a leather swivel chair waits beneath an unlit spotlight. Three people gently emerge out of shadow; two women and a cameraman.

There is a fourth figure, squatting almost out of sight in the deeper shade of office cabinets. Malenga pauses before Tomas of the Nine Lives. She sucks in breath so sharply that the taller woman steps forward, takes her arm.

"Are you all right?"

Bless you, my little brother.

All right now.

"Am I allowed to answer that question, Mr Maynard?"

"What question?"

Celia Bennett says, "I asked her how she was . . . What has happened to her?"

Malenga speaks up for her bruises. "I fell against a Crowbar."

"Crowbar?"

I feel your stare, Tomas.

Maynard: "You can say what you like, Miss Nakale, so long as the film's not running. Get me?"

"I'm feeling wonderful. Look at me. The Boers run the best holiday camps in the world."

"None of that!" Maynard curses his generosity. "Listen, Missy, but for me—"

"Yes, but for you I'd still be up to my knees in shit."

"That's right. Then show some gratitude."

"And when you've finished with me, I'll be back up to my neck in shit. Thanks a million."

Her mind is really on Tomas. She cannot resist giving him a smile, looking him over.

He's grown. Or is it the light? Still got that old dictionary, Tomas?

Of course.

Celia tries to bring matters back to the point. "Just a few questions, Malenga. Whatever you think about these circumstances, we're not party to them. We're here to tell a balanced story."

"Balanced?" More words without meaning. "Do you think that's possible?"

"We try our best."

"Best, yes . . . These people blew the foot off my best pupil. You should've seen the blood. How can you be balanced about that?"

Maynard bellows, "No more of that!"

"Why not?"

"Because it's not part of the story, that's why."

"On the contrary—"

"Be silent!"

She is abruptly calm, icily calm. "So sorry." Maynard

relaxes. "You're right, Mr Maynard."

"Sure. OK then."

"It's not part of the same story. Nor was the burning of my village. Or my friend Doctor Garcia having his throat cut . . . Or my kidnap!"

"Miss Nakale—you've burnt your boats this day!"

"But I was agreeing with you, Mr Maynard . . . And you did give me permission to say what I liked so long as the camera wasn't running."

He suspects her. She is a manipulator; the worst kind of woman, one with brains.

And he needs that film.

"You agree not to say those things?"

She nods. "On one condition."

Insolent little bitch. He admires her nerve but not as much as he resents it. "No conditions."

"At least hear her out, Mr Maynard," implores Celia.

"Well, Nakale?"

"I'd like . . . my cell-mate, Ida, to be taken to the Medical Centre."

"There was no cell-mate—"

"She's taken for interrogation every day. They've wrecked her." She pauses. Maynard's patience is at an end. One more word out of place and she will be thrown back into her cell with nothing achieved.

Malenga's tone is persuasive now. If you're all aggression, the world's a brick wall. "Please—I'm asking for her to be patched up, that's all; and given a decent cell. At least look at her, Henry."

Henry! The American cannot remember the last time anyone used his Christian name; yet he has always considered it a wholesome name, full of friendliness. His face gives nothing away. "I'll make enquiries. But remember, I'm only an observer around here."

Words are on her lips: harsh ones. She glances at Tomas. He is smiling at her. She repeats the words that matter. "My friend's called Ida. She's thirty . . . you'll recognize her because she's only got one arm."

Everybody waits, nobody speaks.

Malenga takes the initiative. "Now I am ready to appeal to my father." She stares at the faces staring into hers. "Oh, I've a question . . . Do I *address* him—" She returns Tomas's smile, "—as a freedom fighter or a terrorist?"

Chapter Nine

Something soft, stroking the air; something fleecy. Could this be another small miracle? Whispering against the corrugated roof, first a sprinkle, a tender greeting from the heavens, almost a murmur of love.

Rain!

Alone now, for Maynard has been as good as his word. How're your white sheets and crisp pillow, Ida? Malenga shudders at the remembrance: suddenly awakened on her first night in the cell—door unbolted, a body propelled across space, falling in sludge, yes, the dust mixed with rotted food, with piss and shit; a woman, head-shaved, face pumpkin-swollen.

Malenga had helped Ida to the single bunk that let down from the wall. Her clothes were in rags. Every part of her was bruises. "But why?"

Too injured to speak. And Malenga had beaten on the cell door for attention. None came. She had yelled through the cell window high above her.

Nothing but silence. "Forget it, Sister."

Her arm and her shoulder had been offered in comfort, and had been welcomed. "I'm Malenga."

A nod. "You're the famous prisoner." A smile through pain. "Your father's always been one of my pin-ups."

In the darkness Malenga felt the sandy texture of dried blood. "Will they do this to me?"

"Your name will protect you . . . Being a Nakale is almost as good as being a white."

"I'd not noticed . . . where're you from, Ida?"

"Up the road."

Smiles help. Jokes are even better—right, Nose?

"I mean it. I was born not fifty kilometres from here. North. No man's land. I was a teacher once. The Boers cleared my village to make it a game reserve—so-called. It's actually an arms route into Angola."

"Why are they doing this to you?"

"I'm Black, aren't I? I'm educated, therefore I'm trouble. Most of all, they want information on my brothers in SWAPO*."

Droplets in the air are wafted across the cell by the rising wind. Up the road. How good that phrase had sounded, how reassuring. "And that's where I'm heading, Sister. Because when those elections happen, if they ever happen, I'm going to be there. Before dawn, with my own pencil in my hand, ready to put down that wonderful cross on the ballot paper —the cross that says, 'Get out!' . . . Like to join me?"

Dreams.

It is lonely now. Existence in the cell had been tolerable with Ida to share it, to exchange life stories as Malenga and Hamish had done on the journey to the Big Man's camp; and such stories had become treasures, richer than uranium, more precious than diamonds.

*SOUTH WEST AFRICA PEOPLE'S ORGANISATION, fighting in Namibia against South African occupation, and shortly to become the elected government of an Independent Namibia.

Up the road. Hear that, Hamish?—we're off up the road.

Is this a kind of laughter?

The Rain God (could this be Wise Choko?) has tired of warnings. His voice is a roll of drums. Like that winter hail on Snowdon once, when we were trapped half-way up. Rebecca refused to stay put. She was found next morning at the bottom of a hundred foot drop. Somehow the rest of us got blamed.

Rain. Sweeping into the cell. We huddled together, that's what saved us. Hug me, Fransina. You were so scared for me after that.

I can almost hear your voice
Above the storm, reminding me
To take my coat, button up tight.
Yet this child has grown too tall
For her forehead to be kissed.
Though not too old to yearn
For the healing touch of your lips.

Cold rain, smarting rain. But drinkable rain, gushing off the roof into Malenga's outstretched palms.

Celia Bennett had protested when Henry Maynard instructed the guards to escort Malenga back to her cell. "You assured us she'd be put in the billets with the women workers."

"I'm not God around here, Miss Bennett. This lot's gun-happy and they're not prepared to let a Nakale, of all people, incite the population to rebellion."

"That's nonsense!"

"And have you forgotten?—she's topped a member of Koevoet. I assure you, these boys aren't the Sisters of Mercy."

"You can help her."

"Miracles are not my business."

Hamish: "The Okavango is full of miracles."

Malenga moves out of the storm, yet keeps watching it, cold on cold.

You're a bit of a miracle, Hamish.

Glad to be of service.

Your dreams touch me.

Out there the saltpans are filling up and the animals are coming to drink: gemsbok, impala, giraffe, elephant; trekking across forests of rain.

Those must be very special glasses you're wearing.

Celia had persisted: "In any event, Koevoet is to be disbanded."

"Miss Bennett, is it because you're a Brit that makes you so innocent? Koevoet is the Devil in uniform, impossible to disband. OK, you put them in a different uniform, give 'em a different name—but killing is their business, and business is good. Always will be."

"And you salute them, Mr Maynard."

"Only if I have to."

You know what, Malenga?

Tell me.

It's the hippo trails that draw in the flood. And it happens before your eyes. The grass suddenly changes colour. The storm-lilies explode, like pink paint. See, kingfishers.

I saw one once, beside an English river; the Stour I think.

Watch the speed of their wings. And look, where the land's still dry—antelope, your zebras. There, see, hyenas squaring up to the wildebeest. They walk as if the world's weighting down their heads.

Hyenas or wildebeest?

Both.

Like the way I feel.

"Sister?"

Malenga hears but does not respond. Her mind is already too full of voices. Rain is coming in through the roof.

Forceful now, "Sister!" Above the pounding of the storm, a shout, "Ma-len-ga!" Around the cell bars from below, a boy's hands. All at once, her fingers clamped over his.

"Oh God, Tomas, they'll shoot you."

A hunting knife is pressed through the bars, handle thrust down towards her. In Tuga, "There's only one guard, dozed off."

"No, Tomas." Not again. No more killing.

Hands heave a face into view. "Sister!" It is all in the word: I've risked everything, don't leave me hanging. He switches to English as though this might carry more weight with her. "Only chance, Sister. Tomorrow—I go. Is all over. Gone!"

The rain is thunder in her head. Maynard said enough: I'm doomed, for Koevoet never forgive. One night I'll be found with my throat cut. Having done the deed myself, of course.

She holds on to Tomas's hand. "Listen, Tomas."

He is saying, "I help your friend too, Malenga." In Tuga again he is describing the Steamer. It has no lock on the outside, only a catch.

She is anticipating fences, barbed wire circled by barbed wire, guards, a machine-gun post—and beyond, open, flat roads constantly patrolled.

She has the knife. You only need to wound the guard. No! "I can't do it, Tomas."

What's it matter? You are already a murderer.

"Call the guard, Sister. You must do it now."

She throws the knife back through the cell window; and at exactly the same moment, Choko speaks. The drenched night erupts with man-made thunder. Beneath her feet the ground moves.

Shells!

Mortar fire screams through darkness. She hears Tomas cry, "Attack!" Malenga remembers the captives being escorted across the drill square.

Ida: "Something's in the air—be ready."

Did they double the guard as Maynard recommended?

"I think we know our business, Mr Maynard."

A massive explosion breaks open the night. Malenga shudders at the noise.

"They come for prisoners, Sister."

The sky is lit by shell fire, the air riddled with rifle fire. The machine-gun post dominating the camp from its high timber tower is struck, topples.

Malenga grips the bars, presses her face against them. The far blockhouse has been hit, is ablaze. Guards sprint in panic across each other's path.

Those heading for the armoury and the ammunition depot halt, retreat, as the biggest explosion of all detonates stocks of shells, mortars, grenades, bullets, flares and finally petrol and oil.

Malenga's door swings wide open. She crouches, ready to spring.

Tomas: "Guard, he varnish!"

"Vanish, do you mean?" Into her arms, clutching, joyful.

"Quick!" The most unnecessary word in the language.

"Hamish . . . Then Ida, Medical Block."

Everybody is escaping. From the women's billets—are

those cheers? Are these unknown warriors their husbands, fathers, sons, brothers?

Some will fall, most will make it.

Hamish has kicked a hole through his door, and his arm is reaching—vainly—up to the catch. Three inches short. He falls on Malenga. "You smell of lavender!"

All around them, small arms fire. Tomas is pushing them. "Scram!"

"Who's this?"

"Son of Choko the Wise One—do as he says!"

Fireworks night. The fence is gone, flattened. The Medical Centre is ablaze. "We've got to find Ida."

Yet Ida finds them before they find her. She comes, staggering, a stick in her hand, held now to steady her, but doubtless used a moment ago to command her escape. "What did I tell you?"

They pass bodies, combatants of both sides. A woman lies dead, ten paces from liberty. But others are down the road, spreading; pigeons fluttering—homeward bound.

Ida permits Malenga to take her arm, steady her, but she waves off Hamish with her stick. "I'm not a cripple . . . yet." She laughs, tilts her head back into the storm, drinks in the sky. "Which way?"

As if we didn't know. Malenga answers for Ida:

"Up the road!"

One of three trucks has lingered in the mud, inviting passengers. "Catch it!" yells Hamish. They are lifted aboard among at least thirty others.

Nobody speaks but the rain. They just feel each other, the joy of it. Take a picture, somebody. Something for keeps. Hamish's arm is around Malenga's shoulder; his other clutches Tomas. He cheers into the storm, salutes the lightning:

"Li-ber-tee!—God, it tastes sweet!"

Ida: "One day of it and I'll die happy."

"Did you see the Yank? He was scuttering around in his underpants."

After an hour's drive at speed, rocking, bumping, skidding, the truck slows. One of the assault squad leans from his cab, shouts at his cargo:

"From here we go alone, comrades!"

Ida presses Malenga's arm. "I smell our front garden!"

They climb down, shout their thanks, stumble together in mud, yet find the strength to hold each other and defy the lightning with a jig of celebration.

Hamish: "Hear what one of them said, Malenga?—'May Africa be free of her chains!' I'll drink to that."

North beyond north, veering westerly as Choko flies, is Angola, the dream. Hamish's hand reaches for hers. "We'll make it!"

On the way there, by a modest detour, is Ida's village. "You can rest in the ruins . . . Come darkness, you'll be able to head for the border."

Off the dirt track, through scrub. The rain has eased. At the outskirts of her village, Ida pauses beside a graveyard in miniature—of tiny crosses tied with hemp. "I've one of mine in there. She was called Nkuli—daughter of liberty." Her face is dry. She shrugs. "Kids die early in these parts."

Morning extinguishes all memory of the storm. Two unpaved streets, meeting at right angles, make up the village. Most of the houses, of adobe walls and corrugated roofs, have been demolished.

"Artillery shells," says Ida, explaining the gaping holes in the walls of the homesteads. "The Boers had really good target practice here."

To the very spot, a corner house, roof collapsed, walls in jagged outline. "*Chez moi*, comrades!" They enter from the rear through a vegetable plot buried under dust. Ida proudly points out the blue-brick fireplace. "Still in one piece!" It was built by her father. "He told me stories, just here. We'd one chair in those days."

"A fireplace in this heat?"

Ida sits, sighs—laughs. "A bit daft—but the nights are cold."

Tomas has been exploring. His cry alerts the travellers. "Water!" The village water pump still operates.

Refreshed, they search the houses and bring together a comforting hoard of tinned foods—beans, pilchards, corn, evaporated milk. Hamish has found a screwdriver blade. With the assistance of a broken brick, he smashes open the tins. "Dinner at the Ritz!"

Midday, and silence, except for somewhere over the horizon, beyond the desert line, the drone of aircraft. "Tonight," Ida has predicted, "if the gods look favourably upon you, you'll reach Botswana. Friendly territory . . . Now you must get some sleep."

To mention sleep is to make it happen. Ida watches Malenga and Hamish. They have flopped together, arms entwined, heads touching. She is amazed, incredulous. "How come this love, Tomas—white and Black?"

But Tomas also floats on the wings of Choko, sleep-giver, curled close to his sister's side.

Ida speaks softly, ominously. "You're going to need all the luck in the world, comrades . . . Plus some."

*

Dusk, and an orange sun ignites defiles of flat-topped acacia. A wind, powerful and hot, carves its rhymes in the far-off sand.

"Here'll do, Chalky. Time for that fag you owe me."

An open-topped jeep, with rear-mounted machine-gun, rolls to a halt beside the kids' cemetery. The corporal reports in over the intercom. "Search Vehicle Bravo-3, making its last call . . . Dodge City looks as deserted as ever. We shall make a quick recce before dark. Over and out."

"It's you who owes me a fag, Corp."

"Don't quibble, son."

Tomas keeps watch, down wind and in deepest shadow. He hears the wistful complaint of the sign above Sam's Superstore, the desert breeze its only customer. He returns to Ida's place, shakes legs. "Soldiers come!"

The jeep steers into the high street, faces south. It is observed by four pairs of eyes from the ruin on the next corner. Tomas has collected missiles—bricks, chunks of concrete, breeze-block, spars of wood.

Some contest: sticks and stones.

The thoughts of Malenga, Ida and Hamish are one. They would rather die than be taken again. Nevertheless, they are sick with disappointment.

"And I thought our luck had turned."

They wait. Cigarettes are being smoked. The conversation of the soldiers, close enough for every word to be discerned in the twilit silence, centres on the topic of cricket.

"True, Corp," says Private Chalky White, "the Springboks never played the Blacks in a Test match. But what if they did, and what if we got the hell beaten out of us—what price racial superiority then?"

"That would be an impossible situation, son. We'd not allow it."

The soldiers need only stand up in the jeep to see the fugitives; the tops of three heads.

Three?

Without glancing towards him, Malanga has reached out her hand to Hamish. She half turns.

Hamish is gone.

No! Please God, don't let him have thought of something.

"How'd we stop 'em, Corp? I mean, in a game of cricket we'd both have to play by the same rules."

"There's where you're wrong, junior. Because in every game there's a set of hidden rules . . . Winners know all about them."

"I'm all ears, Corp."

"Against a side of uppity Zulus we'd apply the HBB rule."

"HBB? Do you mean Leg Before Wicket?"

"No, HBB—Head Before Bullet."

"You're a real philosopher, Corp."

The soldiers have stepped down from the jeep, rifle straps hooked over their shoulders.

Ida: "Where's the boy?"

Malenga is silent.

"Deserted us?"

A blazing whisper: "No!"

"Now I want it thorough, Chalky. No skimping."

"*Every* house, Corp?"

"HBB, son!"

The corporal heads straight for Ida's house. Another few paces and he will make a capture without even going in off the street. He pulls up at a shout from Chalky.

"Corporal! . . . Look, Corp!" He points down the main

street, past Sam's Superstore, sign creaking. "See him?" Gun up, aimed. "White!"

The corporal about-turns. He was a slip-catch away from capturing the daughter of the Most Wanted Man in Southern Africa.

"Easy does it, Chalky, old son."

The length of approximately three cricket pitches away, Hamish Ross stands perfectly still; forlorn, like a fielder guilty of butterfingers. His hands are in the air. He shouts: "Thank God!"

He ventures a step forward, then a few more, his face masked with a convincing smile of relief. "Defence Force?" His stark hands turn into waving hands. "Am *I* glad to see *you*?"

"Don't lower that rifle, Chalky, till I tell you . . . Boy, stay right where you are. Freeze!"

Chalky White is ready to relax and celebrate. "One of ours, Corp."

"Oh yeah? Follow behind, and cover me." The corporal peers ahead of him. "Specs . . . I've half a mind I know this kid."

Ida stands up. "He's doing it so you can get away."

Malenga isn't impressed. "If he thinks we'd desert him—"

"Do it! Don't waste your one chance."

"I've suffered enough losses lately." Malenga grips Tomas's shoulder. She eyes the jeep. In Tuga: "If I drive, can you aim the pop-gun?"

Hamish claims, "They brought me here. After the attack."

"Attack? What attack?"

"On the camp. I was doing guard duty."

Nearer. "We know you, son. Cut the crap."

Hamish recognizes his old training corporal. They called

him 'Run 'em Ragged' because that's what he did. The hands are down, all spirit and hope gone.

"Heap O'Shit, right? . . . My team, Chalky—him and his college-boy mate. How do they thank me?—they up and scarper for the woods. Lost face over that, I did."

Private White has not been paying attention. He cocks an ear, staring out into the twilight, beyond the last village shacks. "Hear that, Corp?"

"Hear what?"

"Traffic—motors."

"Can't be. This dump's out of bounds."

"Well somebody's saying stuff that—listen!"

A rumble. Old engines. Clapped-out sounds, chugging. And in plenty: citizens returning home.

"It's trouble, Corp . . . I mean, just the two of us."

"We've the bloody machine-gun, haven't we, laddie?"

"But—"

"Back to Bravo-3. And take this son of a bitch with you."

For Hamish it has only been a glimpse, but his heart surges. In the dark behind the soldiers, movement, two dartings between Ida's place and the jeep.

He talks for time. "I don't think you understand, Corporal. My friend and I were on a Koevoet mission. We were to kidnap a very important person."

For a moment the delaying tactic works. The corporal is familiar with Captain Mike Hargreaves' speciality: hadn't he snatched a camp full of diamond-mine workers once, and marched them hundreds of kilometres from Angola into Zaire?

It looked great in the newspapers.

"You were with Zorro?"

"Yes, and Cardinal . . . Musso, is he still complaining about his sore leg?"

Chalky White laughs. "Sure is." For an instant the soldiers' rifles are lowered. Hamish plunges between them, sprinting for Bravo-3.

The pursuit never gets under way. "Drop the guns!" Malenga has switched on the beam lights of the jeep. Tomas is visible against the sky. He aims the machine-gun at the soldiers' legs.

"Go on—drop them!"

Chalky obeys immediately. The corporal delays. He has never taken an order from a Black, much less a Black woman. "Do it, Corp, for Christ's sake!"

"Know who that is, soldier?"

"Drop it now!"

"It's the dame who did for Zorro." The corporal casts his gun into the sand.

Hamish gathers up the weapons. "Very wise, because she's FAPLA, one of the youth cadres. The boy fought at Cuito . . . gun-belts too, if you please. And now your pants, Corp."

The corporal protests.

"Yes, your trousers. Mine got mangled in the wash . . . Boots too. Where we're going, folks in bare feet get bitten."

"You're going to hell, kid." The corporal discards his pants, his boots—and his pride.

"Now down on your faces."

Ida has broken cover. She stands beside the jeep. "Kill them!"

Malenga calls to Hamish, holds up a pair of handcuffs she's found under the dashboard. She lobs them towards him.

"Kill them!" repeats Ida. "Or they'll come after you for ever."

The cavalcade of motors has entered the village; Ida's people.

Fingers over the trigger, Tomas asks: "Do I, Sister?"

What Chalky White described as 'traffic' is about to transform the world's most deserted and unpromising village into Trafalgar Square at rush-hour. "What do we do, Corp?"

Old bangers of every sort and shape rattle up the avenue, now starlit, lamp-dancing; vans tied with hemp, heaped to the sky with furniture, bedding; clanking with kettles and pans, clinking with dishes, hoes, spades and tin cans. As soon as the first vehicles in the convoy halt, out flutter hens, down stump pigs and goats, followed by kids of the human variety.

"Christ, Corp—you're crying!"

"I am not crying."

"Bloody crying!"

For a third time of asking, Ida calls for the death of these oppressors of her race, but the spectre of Zorro, which will haunt Malenga for the rest of her days, is their protection. OK, if she really was FAPLA; if she was a Namibian or a Black South African and had suffered at the hands of these butchers—yes, the voice of hatred might drown all others.

"Not this time."

Hamish agrees. "No, not with their pants down."

Malenga shouts: "Go!"

Handcuffs rattling, the corporal and Private Chalky White sprint away from the oncoming traffic, out through the ruined houses and towards the dirt road, west and south.

"It was an entire battalion of armed subversives," the corporal is to report to his superior officer. "Fifty percent of them were FAPLA terrorists from over the border. That means we've been invaded. You've got to nuke Angola, Sir, at once!"

Chapter Ten

"Don't fall asleep. I need you . . . To box the compass."

"Box it?"

"A nautical term. That means all thirty-two points, and then you come back to where you started from."

"A bit like us."

A milk-white moon competes with the biggest skyful of stars ever witnessed by human eye: Hamish's judgment.

Bravo-3 has not only provided them with a four-wheel drive getaway, it has treated them to maps, tools, a water flask, even a first-aid box.

"Too good to be true."

"That was what I was thinking."

"On the other hand, we've been due some luck."

"Very true."

Luck—but very little petrol.

"It'll get you over the border," Ida had said. "In any case, ditch it. As soon as they find Julius Nakale's daughter is on the run with Defence Force property, you'll need Choko the Protector to be on his top form if you're ever to hear the bells of Huambo."

Huambo, yes. It's on my list.

Hamish: "How come you can handle a bus like this?"

"Had a boyfriend in Worcester. He took me stock-car racing. I came fourth in the women's event." A smile. "Ran into a tree on the way home!"

"She also great football star," adds Tomas from the rear. "Only—not good header, but she tackle like crocodile bit your foot."

"Thirty kilometres, possibly less," Ida had judged.

Together they have examined the maps in torchlight. "Meaning, I think, thirty kilometres to here."

"Is there actually a fence?"

"Some sort, to hold back the animals." They drive through bush, chiefly acacia scrub rooted in bone-hard earth. Malenga watches the jeep's headlights read the dark: one word at a time.

This is crazy, the dream before the awakening. So make the best of it. The speed of Bravo-3 has turned the still air into an intoxicating breeze.

I can feel the stars through the top of my head.

Only prisoners
Appreciate
The true joy of freedom,
While the free
Forget
The price of liberty.

A sudden bump, acacia fighting the wheels; swerving, pulling straight once more.

Steady! Dozy idiot. If you fall asleep, you'll kill all of us. Grip the wheel hard, stretch, tense the muscles, take deep breaths. Brain—don't you dare switch off.

Easier said than done. Eyes going doggo. Starlight splashes over white earth. Tree copses looming, skirted.

Orbital desertway.

"After the fence," Ida had said, "there's desert, forty or fifty kilometres of it . . . Botswana's neutral and independent, so you'll be safe. Maybe the San people will help you. Or the lions'll eat you."

Never been eaten by a lion.

But for the military helicopter, the fugitives might have slept till the next century. It breaks open the dawn for them, towing behind it a red sky, tracered with grey; threatening.

Even the young feel in their joints the advancing storm. Noises carry. The smells of scrub and copse spread through the cold, trembling air.

"They've found us."

"It could just be a normal patrol."

The crew of Bravo-3 had fallen asleep within sight of the boundary fence. Beyond is refuge from the vengeance of the Boers. "I should have kept on."

Hamish has cleaned his glasses. He identifies the helicopter. "Alouette. They're not here to spot wild game."

First action: abandon vehicle. For the present it will remain camouflaged—by tree cover, by morning shadow. But the sun is scaling the heavens, pursuing the last traces of night. "Those clouds'll help."

"If they land, we've a chance. We'll go for the fence."

"We have gun," reminds Tomas.

"I don't want any firing."

"They'll be firing at us, Malenga. In this life, you've got to fight back."

"Is killing people the only way to do that?" She is reluctant to argue. "Let's just keep out of sight."

The Alouette has charted a route directly along the fence,

and scrupulously within the border; low, roaring, sun-flashing.

Tomas suggests, "Best we wait for storm. Then much dark. Choko send firelight."

"Lightning." Malenga corrects him as though she is back teaching her village class.

The Alouette shrinks from the size of a raven to a bat to a mosquito.

"Let's eat while we can." In the corporal's mess tin they find cheese snaps, and more fruit cake wrapped in cling-film. "They must have got a job-lot of this half-price."

The water passes from hand to hand. "How much petrol?"

"Don't ask."

"Helicopter return," announces Tomas.

Mosquito, bat, raven—eagle.

Sun up, glinting on metal. "Come on, storm—storm!" The Alouette banks in from the fence. Eagle becomes vulture, scouring the woodland, then rising, slow-wheeling, hovering before diving once more towards the trees.

"They've got to be down there somewhere, Sir."

"OK, hold her steady. See anything, Cardinal?"

Cardinal shrugs. He hates flying. Two more days and he will be out of all this for good.

"There!" The captain is first to spot Bravo-3 among the trees. "Ours all right . . . Abandoned. They won't be far off. OK, Zorro, this one's for you, pal."

A fury of blades, close, descending, almost ringing through the storm-awaiting air: down, the sand beneath the 'copter stirred by a whirlwind, a rehearsal of what in moments will be released by nature itself.

Hamish decides, "We'll only get away in one piece if we kill them."

The Alouette touches down. Tomas breaks his own silence. "Is true."

"No!"

"Why not, if it saves us?"

"Because we'll not have been worth saving."

"That's ridiculous."

"So be it."

"Malenga!"

She refuses to listen. She thrusts Hamish off. She races back to Bravo-3, Hamish and Tomas at her heels. She slings herself behind the wheel. "I drive—so I decide. We go for the fence . . . and I don't want you to use that gun."

"Then they'll pick us off." The ignition is on. "You're being stupid."

"Don't you call me stupid, stupid!"

"We can do without name-calling."

First gear. "So who started it?"

Tomas is trying to say, "Shut up—they hear you!"

"A great time to have our first quarrel."

"You're so stubborn."

"*Silencio!*" bellows Tomas at the top of his voice.

Malenga: "I'll want an apology when all this is over."

Search Vehicle Bravo-3 strays from the shade into giant sunspills between the trees; accelerating now, sand spurting, in full view of the captain, Cardinal and the helicopter pilot.

One hundred and fifty metres from the fence, and clear; three to four hundred from the Alouette.

"Hold on—and pray!"

Sand hard, good grip; fast, but are we fast enough?

Forty metres, thirty metres, fifteen: Bravo-3 strikes the border fence midway between support poles, lifting them from the earth, tearing open half the wire netting to freedom.

"We need another run at it."

"They're shooting!"

"Above our heads—they want me alive." Reversing. "Got to have space." Malenga pulls Bravo-3 full into the sun. She circles north, seemingly heading for the captain and his escort.

"Scatter!" The captain fires on the run. His bullet turns the jeep's windscreen into a blindscreen, opaque, milky, forcing Malenga to heave herself up from the seat to retain a view of the way head.

"Do 'em, Cardinal!"

Cardinal has positioned himself abreast of the helicopter. This is the easiest target of his life. He knows she has recognized him. Instead of firing, he touches his forage cap with four clasped fingers.

Reversing. The engine snarls, evading more fire from the captain and his pilot. Now the bullets are aimed to kill. They burn metal. A wheel is hit, but not the tyre.

Last chance. Foot down, jam it. Grief, it's raining. Fence bends, holds, trembles—snaps. Cheers from the crew.

"Done it!"

And Tomas rejoices. "Storm come!"

In fury the captain turns on Cardinal. "Sergeant Bishop—you had 'em in your sights."

"They're just kids," answers Cardinal.

"You're on Report, as of now, soldier. Now get aboard—we're going after them."

The pilot queries his commander's order. "I got it in the neck last time, Sir, for crossing into Botswana."

"And you'll get it in the neck from Koevoet if you don't."

Cardinal is calm. He speaks from behind the protection of his rifle. "Me, Captain, I think I'll walk from here."

"I'm ordering you to get on board." The captain's revolver and Cardinal's rifle meet eye to eye. "Very well, if you prefer to be court martialled out of this man's army—walk!"

Hurtling. No other word for it. Past high scrub, between the massive trunks of the mokasatsu.

"That bastard," cries the captain, referring to Cardinal above the roar of the Alouette, "used to be an ace soldier. Well I'm going to see he returns to his sick little wifey with less than the shirt on his back."

"Yes, Sir."

If the captain cared to take a look over his shoulder, he would see that Cardinal has also passed through the fence. His way lies south. He stares after the receding jeep. He salutes once more, "You show 'em, Sheba!"

Rain: but more than rain—spiked, venomous snakes; thunder: but more than thunder—the drums of all Africa from the beginning of time; lightning: but more than lightning—the white fire of gunpowder, explosive, SAM missile, stinger, blowpipe, red-eye in whose ceaseless glare of destruction the peoples of an ancient continent had been enslaved, murdered, stripped of their heritage.

The celebration ends. "They're coming after us."

"It's an international border."

"Tell *them* that!"

Momentarily, in her disappointment, Malenga senses the loss of will to fight. At the same instance she feels Hamish's arm around her. It's uncanny, he reads my mood like no one I've ever met.

"Keep going—flat out!" He slaps the side of Bravo-3 as if it were a steeplechaser with one more jump to go before victory. "You were great." He sucks the storm up his nostrils. "Ah . . . *this* is poetry, Malenga."

Ahead, scrubland identical to that left behind, only sparser. She hears herself bark back into the storm, "No surrender!" If these acacia can do it, tell the desert where to get off; if they can squeeze life out of the impossible earth, so can we.

The Alouette is airborne. It crosses into the air space of Botswana. "We've a right to retrieve what belongs to us," says the captain to the pilot. "Did I hear 'Yes, Sir'?"

"Yes, Sir."

"Then what're we waiting for? Switch on the spotlight and let sport commence."

"Here they come."

The wild-tempered wind tears at the roots of shrub and tree, spreads its power through the tunnel of dunes, buffeting the jeep from front and side. "We're hardly moving."

"Know who that is down there, Gerry?"

The pilot shakes his head. "Runaways, that's all I know. Car thieves."

"That's Julius Nakale's daughter."

"ANC?"

"Terrorist. Wanted for planting bombs in Durban, Jo'burg, Queenstown—you name it. Wants all your Zulus to have votes. What you think of that, Gerry?"

"I'm thinking we ought to stick to orders, Sir, and bring her in alive."

"Too late for that."

All at once, a thickening of woodland. Sometimes I wish all trees would grow in lines.

Hamish returns to the forbidden topic. "We've got to use the gun!"

Malenga does not know any longer. She will not stop him, she will not encourage him. She says nothing as Hamish climbs over the front seat, helped by Tomas; as he says, "Now I'll need you to prop me up, Tomas."

Very brave, my lovely: while Tomas props you up, you protect him. Well I'm not going to let it happen. Bravo-3 accelerates where sanity would propose a touch on the brakes.

"At least we've trees for shelter."

Famous last words—the trees are history. Bravo-3 is now fleeing across open plain, pin-pointed by lightning.

A herd of zebra, resembling a river dividing into tributaries, appears luminous in the steely light. According to Ida, there will be hills to east and north.

"Eland, Malenga! Don't run them down. There'll be buffalo too."

I can't dodge, yet I mustn't stay in a straight line. Would a sudden stop help? Maybe the helicopter would over-shoot, but then it would hover: hawk and us, the little metal mouse.

Got to weave.

Should we, though, give ourselves up?

"You're slowing, Malenga."

"I'm thinking!"

"Faster!"

More zebra, lured by the waters of the Delta. Malenga asks Tomas who painted the stripes on the zebra.

"Choko."

"Why isn't Choko coming to rescue us?"

"Choko stay all time in Angola, Sister."

"*Now* you tell me!"

"Easy meat. Captain."

"We'll come in at them nose on."

"They're passing over . . . now switch direction. Good." Hamish swivels the gun, with Tomas clutching on behind him.

Trees, where are you when I need you? The Dembos forests would hide us, every centimetre. "If we can reach the hills . . ."

Out of range of Bravo-3's gun, the Alouette screams ahead of its prey.

"Keep top speed—they're turning!"

A burst of gunfire from the helicopter takes off the top of a solitary mongongo tree. Goodbye the best shade in Africa. A warning, across the bows. Stop. Surrender.

And be taken again to interrogation? Howled at, punched —fondled? No fear—no slowing. Enveloped now in a tidal flow of zebra.

There are to be no more warnings. The Alouette's second gun-burst hits target: bullets in metal, leaving tracer holes across the jeep's bonnet.

Climbing, soaring, circling—returning for the kill.

"Hold me there, Tomas." To Malenga, "Zig-zag to begin with. Left, right—then pretend to go left again but go straight on."

The fuel gauge registers empty, and into the red.

He'll never be able to take aim with all this bumping. Switch left, good. More woodland coming up, but too thin for cover. At this speed we'll hit something for sure, a root, a skeleton picked clean by lion or vulture.

Right; and hold.

"Coming!"

"Straight and steady."

The fight is in her. "Then go!"

Gunfire from the heavens is answered by gunfire from the

earth, deathfire for deathfire—but trees are struck and Bravo-3 is missed. A glow ahead, beneath the deep curtain of lightning. What purple! Rising to reveal distant hills, brown in mist, round-topped.

"Hit its wheel."

"We're within their range, Captain—that was my wheel."

"Steady me, Tomas." There is this breather. The Alouette skims the treetops, banks, enters its dive once more.

Hamish's fingers close on the trigger. Wait. He tries to anticipate the swoop of the helicopter, the flattening out as its wheels almost touch the leaves above him. He fires.

And the fire comes back.

"Got the brat!"

Hamish has stumbled backwards over Tomas. The gun is released. There is blood on it, on the grip, over the butt. "Sister, he hit!" Hamish is all over Tomas, sprawled, covering him, a fleshy shield, yet a weight crushing Tomas to his knees.

"Across my chest." The agony drives off more words.

Malenga brings Bravo-3 to a stuttering halt under trees. She pulls Hamish over the driver's seat. Her hands are covered in blood. His eyes are open. Of the damage to him, she can, for the moment, tell nothing.

That's what comes with playing soldiers.

She springs from the jeep. She has Hamish by the shoulders. Tomas hooks his hands beneath the wounded youth's knees. Hamish can feel the cool of the hands. He can move his head. He tries to raise it, look at her. She pulls him against her own shoulders and chest. She backs. "Higher, Tomas."

"They come back!"

Hamish's blood spills on her face. She eases him down beside the jeep. "No—further away." She catches her breath.

The Alouette comes out of the storm, its spotlight darkening the gloom around it.

Malenga screams against the thunder:

"Leave us alone!"

"Is that enough, Captain?"

"What Koevoet starts, Gerry, it finishes."

The Alouette has climbed once more to diving height. It banks elegantly into a sheen of silver; leisurely now, for the hunter knows he has brought the victim low.

Malenga has laid Hamish on his back. Mustn't move him more than we have to. My heart's climbing out through my mouth.

Tomas thrusts the first-aid box in to her hands. Lid jammed by bullet. Nails dig in at the corner. "Come on, blast you!—not you, love, the box." Open. Contents spill over wet earth.

Suddenly, no Tomas. Looking round, rain in eyes, drops from the trees. Hands wipe eyes, leave blood. "Tomas—get down from there!"

Tomas replies in Tuga. "Now it is their turn."

"Or yours, you little idiot."

Descending, steeply, hovering, yet pausing only an instant before the final attack. The wind from the east is vanquished by the propeller wind from above.

The Alouette shaves the trees, opens fire.

A bullet answers, or is it more?—passing through steel, making way for another. Thunderbolts strike the control, shatter glass, blitz instruments.

Something tilts. Something does not respond to command.

"Pull out!"

For a merciful second, it almost works. The trees remain

below. Almost; then—engine failure. The trees are going, all of them, crashing sidewards, no match for the savage eagle whose wings have failed; taking off the treetops, descending, rolling.

A solitary baobab tree, oldest and grandest of Africa's inhabitants, a city of a tree, a civilization of a tree, halts the eagle's last flight. Its massive trunk is a trek around.

The explosion shakes earth and sky, penetrates the gloom with the flash of fire.

Then the silence; stillness except for the beating of other wings above the arcade of trees: the death-flight of bats.

Tomas stands motionless, gun barrel levelled from sky to ground. The rain beats on his face, but not so harshly. It is softening. He sees the curtain of day-turned-night begin to lift. He climbs down from Bravo-3.

Malenga has covered her eyes. "Go and see, Tomas." He sprints through the trees to the great baobab, which itself has become a pillar of fire. The heat drives him back.

"No chance they live."

Malenga battles with tears. She points at her wounded lover. "Look what they've done to him . . . Tomas, how're we to get help?"

Tomas clasps her face, hugs her, then inspects the jeep. "No good this, Sister." The last gunburst from the helicopter has holed Bravo-3's radiator. At the rear, the last of the vehicle's petrol supply drips into sand. "Done for."

"Like us?"

Tomas of the Nine Lives shoves out his chest. "Not like us, Sister."

"Don't tell me—we'll think of something . . ."

Chapter Eleven

The storm has left no record of itself. Within an hour the landscape is dry. Rain-jewels which flourished in the new-born sun have faded and vanished. Somewhere north, water will be thrusting water on its way, quenching the parched throats of fossil valleys.

The heat has returned with the hunger of a lion.

Hamish is conscious. "Malenga?"

"Quiet now. Speaking will sap your strength."

"Am I going to make it, Malenga?"

"*We're* going to make it, all of us. Now button up that mouth. Let me finish."

Tomas has emptied the toolbox of the wrecked jeep. "We make, how you say?—stagecar."

"Stagecoach. Yes, excellent, a stretcher on wheels."

With a wheeljack and spanner Tomas removes a front wheel to match the spare.

"In Dr Garcia's book they call it a travois." Malenga has torn open Hamish's shirt, blood-soaked. The bullets—two, possibly three—have gone down through his shoulder, right breast, ribs.

While Tomas attempts to detach the steering column of Bravo-3 to create an axle for the travois, Malenga ransacks the first-aid box. She finds sutures, a substitute for stitching. He needs hospital.

Desperately.

"It done." One travois: constructed of motsaudi branches and twine. The wheels are secured on their makeshift axle with the steel clips from jump leads, one placed inside the hub, one outside.

"Very clever, my young engineer. For that I'll help you make goalposts and nets when we get back home."

The cream-coloured flowers of the motsaudi are ripening. Tomas has torn them off, scattering them, only for Malenga to pick them up and place one into Hamish's hand.

"All the blossoms are coming, Hamish."

Tomas points at the shafts of the travois, cut from the longest of the manageable branches he could find. "We hold like two fat ox."

"Oxen, we say." She looks at herself: pompous bore. She grins. "Two thin ox."

They lift Hamish on to the travois. There is blood at the corner of his mouth. Has it been there all the time—did I miss it?

"Listen, Malenga." For one so wounded, his voice is strong. His eyes flicker open. "The San people—they'll help us."

"Just what we were thinking. But don't talk."

"They're very little people. Yet so wise." He seems to know all about them. "They have dances . . . to make sick people better . . . They can even make the dead return to life."

Show me the dance, Hamish, and I will dance it all my days to save you.

Tomas has strapped the plastic water container to the travois, and a small can of oil. "Feed camp fire in night dark," he explains. He adds Bravo-3's wheeljack to the load. "In case of nasty lion."

Heavy, but smooth, wheels laying treadmarks in firm sand. They'll have no need of tracker dogs. Just follow our spoor.

Yes, Garcia—insanity to travel by day; breaking all the rules. But what choice have we?

Through sparse woodlands, through spaces gaping with white heat. In the angular light, chequered with foliage, bees flicker, flies hum; and across the plain, their shapes distorted by currents of vibrant heat, herds of antelope, zebra and giraffe drift in ghostly, insubstantial processions: a frieze from an old picture book.

How much fluid will we have lost? How much *can* we lose, Garcia?

Those hills don't seem any closer. Feet burning, shoulders stinging with pulling the travois. Knees stiffening. Everything aflame. Come, Mister Bushman, dance me the Eland Dance to cure my blisters.

Playing this game, invented by Tomas to make the time go by: target, the next tree; stop, count thirty, on to the next, count fifty; on to the next, sit down for five minutes; on and on.

"Next."

"Got to rest."

"Next."

"Tomorrow and tomorrow and tomorrow."

At last, under the shade of a mongongo, a full halt. Beyond here there is no visible cover. Soon it will be dark. Malenga checks her patient, feels the pulse. Weak.

"He tough like baobab," says Tomas.

Malenga surveys the brown-loaf hills. "Why aren't they getting any closer? They're on the map—they're not a mirage."

"Mirage, Sister?"

"Something you think's real and wonderful, but doesn't actually exist."

"Like peace?"

She shrugs. "Maybe . . . so what now?"

"We build shelter. Night wind bad. Then we make fire. After, I go hunt."

"And me?"

"Keep brother warm."

"And after that, little general?"

"I find San people."

Tonight he will bring spring-hare. They will eat well.

Just the two of us now, Hamish; your hand in mine. That wind's got ice between its teeth. How do you like our shelter? That whistling sound is the breeze trapped among the stacked branches. When the spring-hare's finished, we'll eat the nuts of the mongongo.

I've only just noticed what beautiful hands you've got. She removes his glasses, cleans them on her shirt. Beautiful eyes, too. "Can you see anything without these on?"

"Eyes shut I can see you . . . Malenga?"

"Yes?"

"We've had so little time."

"If you talk, you—"

"I want to." And then he falls silent. She is close, that is enough. The pain's been horrible, with the bumping, the shifting. Now that he lies still the pain is more leaden than sharp. "You and me, though."

It seems to amaze him that she should count him her friend.

"Is that so surprising?"

"I never had much luck with girls. My specs, you see."

"More fools them."

"It was lucky . . ."

"Lucky?"

"Me deserting, then floating into your life like that . . . Fate."

She leans over him. "Destiny even." She brushes her lips against his forehead. She kisses his mouth.

His jaw trembles with the cold. He refuses to sleep. He seems to understand: to fight sleep is to stay alive. "Tell me your poems, Malenga."

"They're too bitter. Not suitable for the poorly."

"Tell them anyway."

She does, and the duration of them speaks of a journey through dark forests, yet lit on occasion by golden light. The poems touch, merge, become the links in a chain of feeling; a caravan of words reaching through forest to desert, from the closed to the open, from the self-alone to self-shared.

"Will you write a poem about me some day, Malenga?"

"I'll try . . . But you are your own poetry."

"Don't understand that." His eyes are ajar, then shut. "I like it, though."

After each poem, she seeks permission to go on. He nods. "I'm OK. I'm going to be OK."

Colder now; his neck's all goose pimples. Build up the fire. She removes her shirt, rolls it, wraps it round Hamish's throat.

"They're so far away, Malenga."

"Oh?"

"The stars. Such distances. All those people!"

"Rest . . . They're stars of hope, Hamish."

"But frightening too, Malenga."

*

At dawn Malenga goes out into the open. In the smooth sand beyond the mongongo she inscribes a message to the skies, a lesson learnt during those precious days in Benguela.

A long straight line: SERIOUS INJURY, announces the rescue code; IMMEDIATE EVACUATION REQUIRED. Nearby, a giant F—FOOD AND WATER NEEDED. She stands in the dizzying power of the sun. She adds X—UNABLE TO MOVE.

She scans the horizon, melting, rippling, shimmering. "Come on, little hunter, where've you got to?"

Hamish has weathered the night, and now he calls. She runs, kneels beside him, wets his lips with water.

"I got that idea . . ." His voice is so faint, yet it is amazing he has lasted so long. Tough as the baobab. For certain. "You've got to leave me . . . You can make it."

She is angry and in tears at the same time. "I've a better idea—you conserve your strength by not trying to get rid of your pal. And don't forget, Tomas didn't track us all this way to lose us now."

He takes her hand. "Then don't leave me till you have to." He is barely conscious. Moments expand in the heat so they seem like hours. "Are we there?"

"The Okavango?"

"Yes."

"Very close. We'll soon be paddling our boat under the stars. The owl and the pussy-cat. White lover, Black lover in a pea-green boat."

"Thought so . . . Can see . . . white pelicans, avocets, teals, plovers—a thousand species, did you know that? And jacanas. Talk. Malenga. Tell me things."

"OK . . . well, talking of talk, to hear your average westerner, you'd think this great continent had only three languages, all of them European—Tuga, Afrikaans and English . . . But there are six thousand languages spoken, which means six thousand . . ."

He is asleep. She lays her head beside his on the travois: babes in the fiery wood, until, abruptly, she lurches to her feet, wrenched from sticky slumbers by the sound of an aeroplane.

It is passing directly above the mongongo.

Up and sprinting into the open, acting before thinking. "Come back!" Waving at the two-seater plane as it circles lazily in the ascending sun. "It's got Red Cross markings . . . Christ! Hamish, a plane." Wave. "Watch my marks, damn you! Coming back, Hamish!"

Dancing. Red Cross. "See us!"

"Is there papyrus, Malenga?"

Papyrus? "Oh yes, lots of it—and a Red Cross plane. It's going to land."

The plane dips its wing as if to read more clearly the runes in the white sand: SERIOUS INJURY. IMMEDIATE EVACUATION REQUIRED. FOOD AND WATER NEEDED. UNABLE TO MOVE.

A great weight of anxiety is shifting; a stone over a dark, imprisoned spring, losing the substance of stone. The spring starts up into the sun and the stone is weightless as a cloud.

Crying—why am I crying? "We're going to be OK, Hamish."

A neat landing, wheels spinning up sand; fast; then taxiing unhurriedly across the X-mark as if to obliterate and defy its admission of helplessness.

Malenga shades her eyes, waits. The plane door swings open, passenger side. An instant before her eyes do, her instincts drag her back from joy.

The stone has crashed back into its old position.

Henry Maynard steps from the Red Cross plane. He has already drawn his revolver, as much to fend off lions as to capture wildcats. He shields his own eyes, mops his brow. He speaks to the unseen pilot. The engine of the plane cuts out.

Motionless, two shadows.

Malenga's hands are clenched. He is not going to take us back. Hamish calls her. "Everything's OK, Hamish." She retreats into the shade of the mongongo. She picks up the wheeljack.

Maynard has advanced. He shouts: "Malenga Nakale?" He keeps his distance. She has killed a man. "There you are . . . Malenga. You took some finding, baby."

Malenga holds the wheeljack across her chest. "Go back, Mister."

"It's OK, Doll. This is a goodwill mission, not what you think."

"Sir?" The pilot has followed Maynard to the giant F in the sand. "She's overheating and losing oil. I'll need a few minutes."

"So get a move on. I already feel like a burnt kebab." Maynard glances past Malenga towards her patient. "Is the kid dead?"

"He can be saved."

"Let's see." The extent of Hamish's wounds is obvious. Maynard gives himself enough distance for his voice not to be heard by the youth. "We've room in that kite for one—you, Miss Nakale. Now listen good . . . Things have changed Your Dad's suddenly the flavour of the month. The Boers are talking—peace is in the air . . . Julius left the United Nations for Africa yesterday."

Malenga's voice is harsh as the desert. "What's that got to

do with me?" She turns, points at Hamish. "What's it got to do with him?"

"You're free. Forget everything. Julius wants to meet with you in Zaire—you'll enjoy Kinshasa."

Loudly now, almost a scream, "I killed a South African officer . . ."

"Were you sentenced?"

"Probably in my absence."

"Not so. There is no record of a Malenga Nakale in the files of the South African Defence Force. Child, I'm saying to you—it's all over. By tomorrow evening you'll be sipping cocktails with your father before he flies on to Cape Town. Over!"

In these parts there have been terrible storms of late, but no hurricanes: not till now; no whirlwinds. Malenga's passion spirals and explodes. "Over? You think—that's it, that we can all be buddies again?" The tears are of rage.

"Look at your handiwork! Look at him . . . I love that boy and look what you've done to him . . . And me, look at me. These aren't tears, they're fire. My life was burnt to the ground—by you and your sort. And you say it's over? You kill my friends, you—"

"Listen, baby—"

"No, you listen, Mister—"

"I can do nothing for that boy. Even if we took him back, pulled him round—"

"Where I go, he goes." The wheeljack is above her head. She is advancing. "Now get out of our lives!"

"No can do, Miss Nakale." Maynard points his revolver at Malenga. "Orders, I'm afraid. You gotta believe me, you have the assurance of the United States government, that you will be safe. And free."

She has had enough of assurances. "I am not going into that thing alive. You'd be advised to kill us both."

"You want to ruin your father's peace initiative?"

"I am about my own business, not my father's. I'll talk to Julius on Angolan soil, with Hamish beside me—or nowhere else." She pauses. As expected, there is no response. "Very well, I'm asking you nicely to get off our patch."

Maynard's left hand, the one whose sole purpose in these climes is to mop the sweat from the rest of his body, offers a support to the revolver in his right hand. "On this occasion, my lovely, I'm afraid might is right."

"Oh yes?" No thoughts now, no feelings—only action. She strides towards the American and past him.

"Here, what the devil?" Maynard's revolver remains unfired.

Malenga approaches the monoplane. She calls over her shoulder, "So the CIA runs the International Red Cross too, does it?"

"Listen, what the—?"

Any instant, she will suffer as Zorro suffered, fall as Zorro fell. She keeps on walking.

"Nakale—halt it, right there!"

"Have you got photographers waiting in Zaire, Mr Maynard?"

"None of your business."

"It won't make a pretty picture, you taking back a corpse."

"I'm ordering you to—now stop that at once!"

Malenga swings the wheeljack. The windscreen of the plane resists one blow, caves in to the second. "That's for Garcia!" The pilot comes from beneath the engine. He sees the side window shatter. "For you, Dédo!"

Maynard fires a warning. It has no effect. And now there

are two targets in his sights, struggling, one the pilot whom he can ill-afford to lose.

The pilot has managed to duck the swing of the wheeljack only to reel back from a downward blow across the bridge of his nose from Malenga's hand, the heel of it, palm tight open.

Smash—through the open door of the plane: instruments; glass all over the place. The pilot lunges after her. Two bodies hit sand.

"Get her!" Maynard shoots above her, still with mercy in his head; at which the ungrateful bitch darts under the body of the aircraft.

This time he shoots to wound.

The pilot blocks her flight. A blow lands, enough to overturn her. He pins her to the wheel-shaft, and from there the journey is groundwards, face down; eyes, nose and mouth crushed into sand.

"Right Sir, straight through the bloody brain, give it to her, Christ Almighty!" He is bleeding over her. "Sir?"

Henry Maynard's attention is no longer focused on the struggle at his feet. He has lowered his revolver. The trees have come alive. They are walking towards him.

FAPLA?

Figures seem to emerge from an eclipse of the sun. Is it my eyes or have these people brought the dusk with them?

Not FAPLA.

Tomas alone carries anything resembling a weapon. His hunting spear is aimed at the heart of the American. He is too close not to miss. Maynard had suspected the boy from the start—too friendly; too clever by half, for somebody so small.

The others surrounding Maynard and his pilot are no taller than the boy. These are the San, Africa's most ancient people.

"Bloody Bushmen!" Their leader speaks to Maynard, firmly, pointing to the sky. "Translate for me, kid."

Tomas repeats the pointing hand. "He say you buzz off in baby eagle . . . go to homeland, own bantu. Do not interfere no more or Mantis chop off your balls."

"Christ, who taught you your English, son?"

Tomas answers proudly. "My sister!"

The pilot tugs at Maynard's arm. "We can make it, Sir. Let's get out of here. These pygmies give me the willies."

Malenga demands the American's gun. She despatches it high into the mongongo tree.

"There'll be plenty more where that comes from, Nakale."

She is close enough to spit at him. She points to herself. "And there're plenty more where I come from!"

Maynard pulls closed the shattered passenger door. He ought to loathe her. She's made me look my age, like I'm losing my grip. "What do I tell your father?"

Malenga glances back at Hamish. "Tell him we've gone sailing . . . I promise him a postcard from the Okavango."

"That all?"

"If he loves me, he'll understand."

Epilogue

School has broken up for the midday rest. Only the older boys defy the heat—or their hunger, the legacy of war—and race across the shadowed soccer pitch, calling for a through pass, cheering at a goal.

The ball has gone in off one of the new goalposts erected by Malenga and Tomas.

Malenga has watched from the high ground overlooking the village, much of it restored now; as it would be whenever bandits came, whoever they were, however much they destroyed.

Like everyone else in the kimbo, she is perpetually hungry. Fransina, you'd not recognize me.

'We will rebuild'. Dr Garcia had suggested the words be displayed over the entrance to the Medical Centre. The sign hangs there now, above the new verandah, burnt letters in wood:

WE WILL REBUILD

From this altitude can be seen, between the last scramble of trees, the blue ridges of the high plain. A lost memory alights in Malenga's mind like a mayfly: Rodrigo's tattoo, on his forearm. Hamish had pointed it out. "That's what I'd like to feel about my country," he'd said. "Maybe one day."

The tattoo read: ANGOLA—LOVE FOR EVER.

For ever, yes. They were Tomas's words too. With his help Malenga had laid two circles of stones, one intersecting the other. Like Hamish's glasses, she'd thought.

Or a pair of handcuffs.

She had engraved Hamish's name, and those of Dédo and Dr Garcia, on a single wooden plaque. Tomas had brought beeswax, rubbed it into the surface.

"Gift of Choko. Now they will fly on his wings for ever, Sister."

Things are not so painful now, for there is the present: the dying, the sickness; a Medical Centre without supplies, without a doctor.

According to western newspapers, peace reigns once more in troubled Angola.

To the sick and dying
Peace rains
As war poured.

Alone in this high place, I open my heart to the past. Here I can talk to you, Hamish. And in the twilight, sometimes, I can see you.

The forest whispers—
Do you hear?
I am your always
You are my
Ever.

I wrote to your Ma today. At least I could put the words together without smudging them with rain. I told her you gave up soldiering for discovering; that you reached your

Okavango. Well, a slight exaggeration. But the breath of the Okavango, yes, we shared that.

Those children still with the strength to run have gone down the track towards the river, to the new bridge: special guests—the recently-appointed District Manager is to make his first visit. They used to call them Commissars; I wonder why they've changed the name.

Celia: "I promised you we'd get your side of the story, Malenga."

The film crew stay silent, but they are shocked at the sight of her, so thin, so eye-sunken; her beauty gone.

"How did you know where to find me?"

"Maynard told us—who else? Strange sort of fellow. Pops up everywhere. Last time was in Luanda itself! Now he's in South Africa . . . They've just released Mandela, did you know?"

At last, Hamish, something to celebrate. Now you can begin to be proud. To Celia, she says, "So Maynard will be up to more mischief."

"He was full of admiration for you, Malenga."

"Mandela?"

A laugh; all laugh, relax. "Maynard. He said, 'If she can survive the Koevoet, the CIA and the Praying Mantis, she'll survive anything, pass Go and collect two hundred dollars' . . . What did he mean, Praying Mantis?"

Malenga glances down at Salu, Dédo's brother, fixed to her as if—as if with invisible handcuffs. She asks, "Salu, isn't that the story I'm going to tell you this afternoon?"

"Yes, story of big wise Mantis."

Mandela is free: I can permit myself a spoonful of joy. Now's your time, Julius. May Choko be with you.

Celia brings a message from Fransina: Luanda at Easter,

destiny permitting. Malenga shakes her head. "I'll probably not be leaving here. Not yet. Please explain . . . But Tomas will be able to see her."

"He's no longer here?"

"Gone to the capital, to study to be an engineer."

"To build bridges?"

Of course.

"He's promised our football pitch its own floodlights one day . . . That's if we ever get electricity!"

Celia puts voice to her concern about Malenga. "You look so ill."

"I work long hours."

"It's more than that."

"I'll survive. Nakales always do. But I'd appreciate one favour. When you tell our story, tell it straight. This whole nation is starving, it has nothing . . . except hope, and each other. South Africa's done this to us. America's done this to us. The only peace they seem to be interested in is the peace of the dead."

The fire of anger restores her beauty. "Your lot are cooking up deals that scare me more than Zorro ever did."

Celia says, "Then you'll not be too surprised to learn who your new District Manager is . . . Remember Captain Roberto in the Big Man's camp?" She gives a shrug, as if to say—this is the way of the world. "He's your new boss. He was given amnesty and fixed up with a job."

Malenga's smile disguises her feelings. "Then he'd better watch his language."

The film crew are to record the arrival of the District Manager. He will open the Medical Centre which he and his kind destroyed.

"I'll be in school," Malenga decides.

Celia gives her an affectionate but uneasy hug. "Peace is what counts, Malenga."

Does nobody understand?

Malenga gazes beyond Celia's shoulder towards the river where, once upon a time, not many leagues from here, a dinghy floated into the reed banks and into her life; where a Moses rose, wounded and delirious, from the bulrushes: yet carrying an innocent hope—and love.

Yes. Hamish understood.

Malenga hears herself quoting Leon Garcia. "My friend the Cuban doctor believed there are two kinds of peace, the peace of profits and the peace of love." Celia is already down the path. "Which is it we're to be allowed by the Masters, Celia?"

Celia waves but does not reply.

The school bell sounds. The juniors have eaten for the day—one small bowl of maize porridge. They have enough stamina to clap their hands for a story.

Malenga goes down through the trees. Hers is a deep sadness, most of the time tucked out of view, beneath a calmness as still as Lake Nagami.

We never did see the Okavango, Hamish. He is walking with her through the trees, feet leaving tracers of light. The sunset, that's what I want to see, Malenga. More than anything else—the gold and scarlet, in the heavens, in the lakes, while the reed islands prick the light like . . .

Like?

A black scrubbing brush—you're the poet, not me.

I'm not sure of that any more.

Are the night lilies out, Malenga?

Hundreds and thousands.

What colour are they?

Any colour you like—bright blue, pink, yellow. And when the breeze catches them, the upturned leaves flash purple and emerald green.

Storks, are there—and heron?

I can see a chameleon in the motsaudi.

Feeding off the dragonflies?

You can see it?

Yes, yes, I can now. I can see it all.

And the stars, can you see them?

Stars of hope?

"A story, Miss, a story! The one you promised—about the beginning of the world."

"Not till I can hear West Wind whisper in the grass . . . Good. Well, this is the tale the San people told me."

"The San rescued you, didn't they, Miss?"

"Oh yes, but they say it was really the Great Mantis saved us. He sniffed our sweat in the desert . . . Let's go back millions of years, to when the earth was covered by the sea. Here's Mantis—go on, swim like the Mantis.

"Exhausted, worn out with swimming and swimming and swimming, he is about to drown. Yet he has the life of the future within him. And what does he see, flying in the heavens just above his head?"

"The bee, Miss!" shouts Salu.

"He calls out, 'Bee, can you help me—can you fly me to dry land with my precious cargo, with life itself?'"

Malenga looks into the faces of the children; faces drawn tight with hunger, some with fever—lives as fragile as that of Mantis before Bee rescued him. Yet at this instant the upturned faces are bright as the leaves of the lily. A little bit of luck—oh the smallest honeydrop—and these will be the faces of the future.

"Kind Bee does just as she is requested." She? Why not! "She lays poor Mantis down in the heart of a night lily."

I can see them opening, Malenga. It's a miracle, isn't it, them choosing the night-time to come into flower?

"And through the soul of Mantis, the seed of the first human being was planted, the first of the San people. Now do you know what the San call their hills, the ones they've lived among since Bee rescued Mantis?—they call them the Bracelets of the Morning."

That's something else we must see, Malenga—the way dawn sparkles over the granite. And when I've explored all that, I want to go away. Be useful in life. How about you?

Useful? Oh yes.

"Did *you* see the Mantis, Miss?" The child who asks the question has no hand to raise; another victim of mines inscribed Front Towards the Enemy. "Did it talk to you?"

Until Malenga's return, the child—who belonged to no one—had been the child without a name.

"More than that, Nkuli." It had been Malenga's choice, in memory of Ida: Nkuli, short for Nonkulule ko, daughter of freedom. "The Great Mantis was feeling generous in his old age. He offered us three gifts."

"Presents?" Salu asks.

Malenga's voice falls softly against the wind. She can touch the silence. "First, was love. Second, remembrance."

"And third, Miss?"

"The knowledge of what is precious in this world."

The children nod as if no further explanation is required. They gaze at the face which fights back tears.

"That is my story."

Not the first chapter; not the last. And it is also the story of those whose lives were casualties of hope, yet stars of hope, in this war-desolated land; this beautiful land.

But frightening too, Malenga.

Tears now: Hamish, you'll think of something.

One day things will change, even in my own country.

Even there, even now.
The bee circles above my head,
The light sings through her wings—
No surrender.

In the lily's heart,
Mantis stirs:
Everything is to be a beginning.